Bureaucracy of Future Potential

Aaron Zweig

For information on requests for permission to make copies of any part of the work, or to contact the author:

www.AaronZweig.com

Lulu Publishing Enterprises: 860 Aviation Parkway Suite 300 Morrisville, NC 27560
 www.lulu.com
Copyright ©2004

Requests for permission to make copies of any part of the work should be sent via email to:

AaronZweig@mac.com

Library of Congress Cataloging in Publication Data Zweig, Aaron, 1978 -
Bureaucracy of Future Potential
    Title TXu-1-059-224
    ISBN 978-0-6151-4417-7

Other Novels by Aaron Zweig:
Peeling Apart

The greatest contribution Americans
have made to the English language
is the acronym, and yes,
we need at least one more.

Food Delivery

The young adolescent brings a sheet of paper to his elder co-worker with confusion in his eyes. It is a late Friday afternoon, and receiving papers at such an hour is unheard of to a young adolescent who impatiently waits for Friday night partying to begin. Working in a food warehouse and making deliveries to restaurants is all well and good, but not when it interferes with important social engagements. He holds the paper to his face, reading it in mocking tones, seeking a sympathy he will not get.

He reads the paper to his elder co-worker, "we just got this from the Homestead Restaurant. It doesn't say anything about which lettuce variety, amount of seeded buns necessary, or quantity of live lobster demanded. Just an open order marked with extreme urgency, received after 7:00 on Friday night. Don't we stop making deliveries at 5:00? How can one restaurant keep us open beyond normal work hours?"

The young faced adolescent child of the boss's sister exclaimed as he looked over the order sheet with an enigmatic grin and swirling eye. After all, the stated business hours of the Marshall Warehouse clearly state deliveries to terminate after 5:00 on Friday.

"Green leaf, 12 pounds, and three dozen. Put this order together and let's get it over to the Homestead. We have to do it, and I don't want to stay here later than we have to. The Homestead calls in late orders on busy nights, and yes, filling late orders is part of our job description. It's in the back of the brochure, under implications of implied expected loyalty. The Homestead is one of our biggest customers, and if we don't serve them, the account would be lost and our company would suffer. Let's get the order together and move it on out, because the night ain't gettin' any earlier", came the emphatic reply of the older scruffy gentleman with a missing tooth and an odor from his armpit.

The young adolescent shook his head and began to do what his scruffy, toothless, senior co-worker instructed him to. The Marshall Warehouse is quite large, and gathering food items can be relatively time consuming across a large space. But with an inspiration to work efficiently, the adolescent moves much faster than normal. The restaurant product delivery business is a challenging kind of occupation, combining a passion for customer service with a slight distaste for regular work hours. Sunrise to late-afternoon, Saturday, holidays, and the omnipresent potential of filling late urgent orders from a favored client. People who do not have this passion or slight distaste do not last long in this highly competitive business.

The adolescent returned from his journey across the large warehouse, carrying all three items in their appropriate quantities. Three very different items forced him to all corners of the warehouse, starting in the vegetable cooler on the west side, the freezer on the north side, and the lobster tank in the lower half of the new addition. Young, energetic, and inspired to spend time with his comrades, he was able to accomplish his tasks in a third of the time normally expected. The adolescent's speed on this night would come back to haunt him, however, as the scruffy senior would now expect this level of efficiency from this moment forth.

The adolescent begins to speak again as the scruffy senior checks over his work, "here we are in New England, the southern coast of Maine, and we get our lettuce from the fields of California. I can name at least ten farms in this town who could supply us with lettuce, and yet, we have to go thousands of miles away to get what we need. The baguettes are from a factory in Wisconsin, bread probably pulled from the oven more than 18 months ago. Good thing we still have our live Maine lobster to keep us rooted in the community".

As the young adolescent began stacking boxes inside the truck, the scruffy senior replied, "our trading system is volatile to price fluctuations, and based on monetary efficiency, not local community. Now get these boxes on the truck while I warm up the engine. I don't like standing in the rain, so let's do this as fast as we can. I don't care where these food products are coming from, just get them to where they are suppose to go. The system is set up for you to participate, not procrastinate. Let's make our lives happier, our boss appeased, and our customers satisfied. Start loading while I warm".

He scratched his beard and ran for the truck amidst the pelting rain. Pulling away from the loading dock of Marshall Warehouse, the truck blazes through steady rain and moderate gusty wind. The delivery truck parks itself adjacent to the service door of the Homestead kitchen. The adolescent sits back and finishes the conversation discussed during the truck ride, "The computers were down and I couldn't get a hold of her. And she blamed me for not trying, as if it was impossible to believe computers could be down at any given moment. She wouldn't believe me, but she did believe the computers. I wish I was a computer, because then I would have legitimacy to my name".

Uninterested in the end of their conversation, the scruffy senior restated his priorities upon arrival at the Homestead Restaurant, stating, "here we are. I'll go in and take care of the paperwork, you unload the food. Try not to say too much to the guys in there, they're busy and don't want to talk with you. They have a job to do, and so do you. I don't want you getting caught up in mindless chit-chat with line cooks and dishwashers". He raised his odorous arm to exit the truck, moving rapidly to avoid the pelting rain.

The service door of the Homestead swung open, and the society within the walls of a bureaucracy were exposed. The two deliverers scurried apart from each other to fulfill their respective duties; one to obtain a signature from the chef, the other to unload the truck. Needless to say, the service door to the kitchen swung shut almost before it had a chance to swing open. The order was complete, their evening had come to a close. No mindless chit-chat to distract product delivery from its destiny.

They climbed back into the truck, driving home through pelting rain to pursue those important social engagements.

Sinew Money

The Homestead Restaurant was busily working on a busy Friday night. As soon as the delivery items were delivered, the chef's voice rang throughout the kitchen.

"Lobsters, lettuce, and bread arrived. Cover the lobsters with seaweed, cut the lettuce up for tonight's salad, and get the bread onto sheet pans. A book is lost in the library if not properly stowed, as is a Maine lobster if not covered with seaweed at the bottom left corner of the walk-in refrigerator. A library cannot function without order, and neither can a restaurant kitchen. Priorities, people. Establish efficiency of order", came the commands from the chef himself.

As Chef Gregg's voice echoed throughout the kitchen, the cooks came forth to perform their tasks. Scott and Wendy both began working without any hesitation. Lettuce cut for salads, bread stacked on sheet pans, lobsters at bottom left corner covered in hydrated seaweed. Each product had been delivered to its appropriate location for the ease of finding them later, just like a library book in a large library. The grill cook needs to find lobsters in a split second during the dinner rush, the salad cook needs to find chopped lettuce without delay, and bread pans need to be placed in the oven with nimble speed.

Not struggling to instruct workers under a vicious whip, Gregg guides his kitchen staff with a soft hand of confident independence. Many chef's are not cable or secure enough with themselves to act with soft hands in their kitchen, if only because soft hands require a virtue many cannot achieve. Most chef's will avoid confident independence if only to support their ego and self image, but of course, any virtuous chef knows the exact opposite to be true when supporting both ego and self image.

Gregg has his kitchen running like a well oiled bureaucracy, using technology to supplement the human ingenuity needed to make a kitchen successful. Any business of ideas would be a stark and bleak endeavor if human ingenuity were not actively incorporated into bureaucratic dynamics. Gregg understands the presence of humans in his kitchen, but is often led astray by the pressures of political economy and monetary dogma. Gregg is sensitive to these issues, but the pressure from business authorities is often too much for him to handle, and further concessions to the political dogma of monetary pressures is too overwhelming to fight.

It's 7:15 on a Friday night, and the very last possible delivery arrived from the Marshall Warehouse. Hopefully the Homestead will not require any more deliveries, if only because no more are available until tomorrow morning. Gregg called the order just in the nick of time. The entire dining room is seated with paying customers, and the kitchen is scurrying to satisfy all their desires. There are a total of ten workers in the kitchen: 3 line-cooks, 1 salad cook, 1 pastry cook, 3 dishwashers, a chef, and a sous-chef. A good crew of workers, a good bonding of different personalities, a wonderful ensemble of food production.

Chef Gregg always likes to sing while he's working, especially while he's dicing onions. It covers up the tears he is trying to hide as he dices. He begins to sing across the kitchen, "the people, the people, the people. We are here to serve the people, not to delegate our own version of a theocracy the people do not wish to have shoved down their throats. We cannot allow the money of a republican democracy to become our deity, nor the ideology of a political economy become our house of worship. Our people will eat using the fork of free will, not the force feeding spoon of a strong armed dictatorship. Our menu was created on a set of ideas with the use of well informed highly paid corporate consultants who study preferences of the people. Research, my comrades, research. Our kitchen is a well oiled bureaucracy with the pride of the United States of America, balancing both humanity and technology with well informed research. Serve your kitchen well, serve the people well, serve your country well. Of the people, for the people, and by the people; that is what this kitchen stands for. A more perfect union of people and food".

Dicing onions can be a very emotional time in a person's life, with the excess crying coupled with highly demanding focus and skill. Gregg's eyes welled up with tears as he sung the last verse of the kitchen song. Everyone in the kitchen smiled and giggled as they listened to the dedication Gregg has toward his kitchen and country.

The kitchen crew works with a valuable confidence behind them, a confidence guiding them through difficult moments of kitchen work. Not only is kitchen work physically challenging with its cramped spaces, sharp utensils, slippery floors, and screaming hot appliances, it can also take the spirit out of the most talented cooks. The excess hours, low pay, and constant stress of serving hungry people can be demoralizing. Maintaining a cook's confidence and happiness can be enormously challenging, which is why being chef is no time to flutter or flake. It is a position calling for confidence and dedication, soft hands and a slight distaste for normal working hours.

Out came the objectionable voice of Robert, the Jamaican dishwasher carrying a stack of clean dishes across the kitchen. He objects to the singing of his chef, replying, "you sing off-key, just like your people. A nation of singers with sinew voices and no harmony. Loud shouting. People are forced to listen when clamor beats their ears, if only because they have no choice. It is a tragedy of our human condition that clamor can drown passion, withering the beauty of talents. Overwhelmed ears cannot hear the breath of wisdom. Clamor not ceasing will never catch its breath."

Robert ought to be a bitter middle-aged man, but walks with a smile on his face and a laughter contagious to all around him. Working in a Jamaican business firm over the last 20 years, he has made more money washing dishes in Maine for one summer than 10 years worth of salary in Jamaica.

American money sings with a sinew voice, and it draws people from across the world to relocate their homes even if just for half a year. The U.S. has thrived on its own song, humming the tune for the world to follow since its victory in World War II. Untouched by the war on its home soil, untainted by excessive casualties, and primed to benefit from the ignited economy of delivering war products. The world's song was now sung by the Americans, and the new American bureaucracy molded to its tune. And Jamaicans were relocating themselves to Maine, sacrificing a life in Jamaica to be a part of the sinew choir.

American food culture in post WW II developed itself around the economic values of profit margin, shelf-life, and efficient delivery. The advent of Wonder Bread, Twinkies, and processed bologna struck their significance not with exceptional new flavor, nutrition, or community, but with financial gain. Clearly the taste of these foods is repugnant at best, enough to make a mouth snicker with disgust and a stomach churn when trying to digest the excess chemicals, preservatives, and color dyes. To compensate for repugnant taste and difficult digestion, American food producers added addictive agents and catchy slogans to ensure profit margins would remain optimal even in the most recessive of economies.

A grueling dilemma was set in motion between American culture and passionate cooks. A struggle ensued between the tastes of the people and a passion for the culinary arts. Not inclined to seek organic vegetables, fresh bread, or enhanced mustard, the American consumer has been content and comfortable masticating Twinkies and ingesting carcinogenic addictive agents. People want what they like, and all too often, the people like their Twinkies. And this liking of Twinkies has made life difficult for those who pursue the artistry of food, for those who try to change what the people like. Even when what the people like can and will kill them.

Passionate food is largely discouraged in the US for its increased labor requirement, the loss of revenue by processed food distributors, and apathy towards the courage of culinary artists. Battling between passion and American food bureaucracy is a battle fought few and far between. Rare to find is a passionate cook, even more rare to find is passion put into actualization. Food passion is lost when not baking fresh bread, filleting a whole fish, or serving fresh vegetables when nobody cares or can tell the difference. Predictable profit margin is much more aligned with the values of a bureaucratic system. Preservatives, dyes, and chemicals ensure the lessening of each culinary battle and a more glorious outcome for food cost.

When a chef can't sell a piece of food he paid for, it is a loss without reconciliation. Money thrown into the garbage disposal, money thrown into the pits of poor business management. To an American chef, food loss is the equivalent of military insubordination. Don't ever mess with a sergeant's rifle, and don't ever mess with an American chef's food cost. Each will result in a fragmenting end to an otherwise trivial relationship.

Gregg could not foresee a battle of food passion being fought in his very own kitchen, within his very own kitchen staff. Gregg is a dedicated man to the ideology of profit margin, system efficiency, and service of the people, and had not recognized one of his more reserved line cooks as a martyr of passion. Unbeknownst to co-workers in his professional environment, Ebbi lived his days with a seething passion for food. Loving the process of food preparation with delicate confidence through culinary artistry, Ebbi created an outlet for passion few have achieved.

In his professional environment, Ebbi prepares food just as the chef instructs him without complaint of its bland flavor, frozen nature, or excessive chemical composition. Ebbi is a reluctant complier to the powers that be, if only to preserve his employment. Ebbi never attempts to inspire passion to his co-workers or chef. Compliant in following convention for what it's worth, Ebbi yearns for nothing more out of his occupation than wages. Society's competency often sings a song much more sinew than the beating passion of Ebbi's palate, and Ebbi has always conceded. Gregg could not foresee beating passion in his kitchen, could not recognize the improbable diamond cooking under his nose. Although the battle between passion and American bureaucracy can be a grueling and often fruitless endeavor for passion, a victorious passion will one day sparkle its way across the world into eternity.

But no one is quite sure when it will happen.

The Root of Delicious Food

Growing up in a small house outside Portsmouth, New Hampshire, Ebbi learned the eternal balance of water and earth through daydreaming and dilatory sleep. Understanding the universal balance of all things natural became a foundation for all philosophic endeavors to come. Food is a metaphor of the earth and water we ingest to maintain our salubrious existence. Food is the metaphor of life.

Ebbi works his job at the Homestead, passing time away infusing blanched basil leaves with olive oil, preparing tomato emondees, and skimming chicken fat into more edible forms of soup broth. It is here he finds himself, away from the clamor of a complicated society. Ebbi works in bureaucracy as a way to make money, but not as a vehicle to express his passions. Ebbi chooses to save his passionate energy for family and friends.

Ebbi manages to cook food at home for he and his family, growing a small multitude of vegetables in his garden and fresh herbs on the window sill. Without his expressive passion at home, Ebbi would not survive, for passions repressed lead to an untimely and premature death. He must concede to the conventions of society and work to live a life free of homelessness, hunger, and loneliness. Leading a life of homelessness, hunger, and loneliness leads to an untimely and premature death as well, but certainly more uncomfortable than repressed passion.

Ebbi has come to love his job, even though it prevents him from realizing dreams. He enjoys the friends he works with and the required tasks of a cook, enjoying the food handling he would otherwise not have access to. Where else could he dress a rack of lamb or emulsify a raspberry vinaigrette? Certainly not in a high rise office of New York City or a rubber warehouse in Ohio. He is content with sacrificing some passion for the rewards of an occupation, but yearns to combine the two in due time. He is not able to cook the food he would serve himself at home, but he is also not exiled into the back country of anonymity to escape taxation, rent, and culture if he were to go unemployed.

The Homestead menu has proven to be a financial success for over 45 years, and remains resistant to change. Serving food to the same clientele, the menu thrives on bland monotony and predictable routine. Although a passionate rejuvenation of the menu would progress their community's culinary imagination, it is much too risky a financial venture for the Homestead to consider. Customers like what they expect. Passion is risky to bureaucracy. Ebbi goes about his job tasks, following instruction, without raising a heretic voice of inspiring words.

Food is the metaphor of life. If food is bland and tasteless, so be a human's communication. If food is ignored, so be human understanding. If food is rotten and neglected, so be a human's physical and emotional health. Ebbi takes great pride in his food to ensure the metaphoric health of he and his family. If individual humans are preserved with metaphoric health, so goes the family. If families are preserved in metaphoric health, so too will society follow. Food is the metaphor of life. Metaphor is the root of future potential. Metaphor is the root of delicious food.

Naked Invisibility

"I've got an extra insert of salmon down on my end. You can take it because I have another backup ready to go. I filleted three whole fish today, so we have more than enough to go around", Ebbi said as he glanced down at Kendra before returning to his work. Ebbi knelt down into his lower cooler, grabbing the salmon and handed it to her.

"Thanks. I thought we were missing them because I couldn't find them", she replied after accepting the salmon into her grill area.

The business of the night was in full swing, as Friday nights usually are at the Homestead. The busiest and most profitable day of the week, Fridays require working not only efficiently but accurately, as the kitchen staff puts an emphasis on quality and speed to satisfy both the customer and profit production. The more expeditiously a table eats their food and pays their bill, the faster another customer can sit down and partake in the same routine. Maximizing profit by serving food not only in a delicious fashion, but a timely one to satisfy financial lust.

"My sisters could be so horrible to me sometimes, but it's a good thing I can laugh about it now. If I couldn't laugh, I don't think I would be able to cope with the pain childhood has rendered me", sous-chef Wendy exclaimed as she put the finishing touches on a smoked sturgeon platter for a banquet in the green room.

"Sisters? Let me tell you something about brothers. You don't know what its like having two older brothers who embarrass you in the schoolyard in front of peers, exposing your underwear for all to see. Or wearing hand-me-down clothes from many years past, clothes having no fashion or sense of dignity. I never got the chance to purchase new, I was always forced into wearing recycled garments.

It wasn't until I moved out of my parent's house that I was able to buy clothes from the store", replied Chef Gregg.

"I wish I had siblings. You lose so many great stories from childhood when you don't have brothers or sisters to share your time with. So many great insights into the character developments of your own personality are exposed by siblings", Kendra said as she flipped a filet mignon on the grill. Medium rare. Dust with salt and pepper.

Ebbi broke into the conversation as the haddock started to sizzle in his sauté pan. "I love both my sisters and one brother. We make sure to spend every Saturday with each other at my parent's house. I had the most wonderful childhood a kid could have, and my siblings were a big part of it. We never embarrassed or stripped dignity from each other. We still reminisce over our past history together; the trials, tribulations, and joys of life. My siblings are my lifeblood. Without them my spirit would suffer atrocities beyond my comprehension, for my siblings are the metaphor of my own spirit", Ebbi added as he dusted the exposed side of the fish with salt and pepper.

"What made your sisters so horrible, Wendy? What did they do to make you say such a thing about them?", inquired Chef Gregg while he sliced fruit for the buffet tray.

"Well, nothing in particular, really. Just a general stress and pressure from them to be a certain way. This caused many conflicts between us over the years. They still look down on me for not being a corporate lawyer, look down on me for choosing the restaurant business instead of the stock trading business", Wendy replied as she cut rye and pumpernickel bread slices to be arranged around the smoked sturgeon.

"They don't enjoy and respect food? Are you to say your family does not honor the timeless magnificence of food preparation? How could they not be proud of a sister who wants to dedicate herself to the world's oldest art form?", the inquisitive chef inquired of Wendy's family ideology.

"No, they don't honor and respect food preparation. Food is just something to put in your mouth as a way to prevent death by emaciation. They see food as an obstacle of feminine image, and the preparers of food to be shunned with contempt for being part of the

working class. They live in Atlanta and Chicago, and expect laborers
to perform the work they find contemptible. They see food
preparation as the toiling of the poor, a toiling unbecoming of
corporate executives. Oddly enough, neither one eats very much.
They frequently starve themselves even though they possess copious
amounts of money and generous access to food. They never decided
to have a family of their own, falling in love instead with financial
aspirations", Wendy answered as she stacked a pyramid of capers and
sunny half-moon lemon wedges.

Simone overheard Wendy's conversation and said, "I went to
Chicago once. Got me a bratwurst and a pretzel before getting back
on the train. Best bratwurst I ever did have, the second best pretzel I
ever had. New York City still reigns supreme in the pretzel making
business, hands down, no contest. The bread of New York makes my
mouth water just thinking about it. I'd give the prize of greasy meat
to Chicago, but New York is forever the champion of kneaded flour
and water." Simone painted a garnish for the blueberry cheese cake.

"Stop talking about food, you're making me hungry. I'm
hungry and surrounded by food I can't eat, and a mountain full of
work in front of me. Nothing worse than being surrounded by food
you can't eat. Like being at a pretzel stand in New York without any
money", as Kendra flipped her medium well New York strip steak.
Brush with olive oil.

"Hey Doug, we should go down to Boston and get some
chowder on Wednesday. The Red Sox are playing, maybe we could
go to the game. Chowder, beer, and baseball. A fine summer day
spent if there ever was a fine summer day to be spent. It's good to be
an American, its good to be in Boston ", Scott shouted across the line
to Doug.

"Boston sounds great. I haven't been to Fenway since last year,
and the Sox lost the game. We need to go and get some oysters while
we're there, to indulge in fine seafood cuisine. Hey, maybe we'll see
that beer vendor again with the flapping tooth", Doug responded as
he placed a dollop of balsamic dressing on a house salad. Sprinkle
with salt and pepper.

"I'd invite Ebbi to come along with us, but he doesn't like to
eat dairy food. Sorry pal, this is a chowder only party. Either you're

in, or you're out. We can't have someone in our group not complying to conformity", Scott spoke his words toward the lactose intolerant sauté cook.

"I don't have Wednesday off, anyway. Besides, I have to help my sister lay hardwood floor in her house. I love baseball, though, and would love to go with you guys sometime. And the last time I checked there wasn't a three cheese minimum to get into the ballpark, conformity boy", Ebbi replied as he threw eight large shrimp into a pre-heated pan for scampi.

"Did your sisters ever want you to become a corporate lawyer? Did they ever pressure you to follow a different career path than the culinary arts? Did your sisters attempt to squash your passions with critical judgment, or did they badger you with demeaning advice?", Gregg asked as he knelt down to fill the dressing bowl for the vegetable platter.

"When I told them I would rather go to culinary school than Yale Law they wouldn't stop yelping and cawing at me. Mentioning to everyone we knew I was to become part of the abominable working class. After I left to pursue my passions, I never thought I could show my face again n Connecticut, let alone my hometown of Stamford. So I moved to Maine, where I could be respected for the craft I dedicated my life to. At the very least, nobody knew me here, and I could surround myself with a conformity that appreciated my passions for what they were", as Wendy dotted cream cheese in artistic circuitous swirls with a single caper on each.

"I never encountered those problems. My father had been a military man his entire life and learned to respect the institution of food preparation. Never does a military man take for granted the food he is served. The food may be of horrible taste and low quality, and the soldier may drench it in Tabasco sauce or ketchup, but never do they take it for granted. The backbone of any military effort, the troops must eat. My father patted me on the back when I got my first job at age 17 in a kitchen. 'Serve your country well' he said. 'America is the breadbasket of the world, and may the breadbasket live forever'. Joining the restaurant business was a patriotic act in his eyes, and one my father is still proud of. No other duty is greater to a country than providing food for its citizens", as Gregg lifted his vegetable tray onto the rack and into the walk-in refrigerator.

"I'll tell you something Scott, the chowder might be good in Boston, but so is the seafood. We really need to get some oysters, haddock, and tuna while we're down there. We'll have the ultimate seafood feast, complete with every creature and plant that thrives in the water. Boston will never know a feast like ours again, for we will indulge until we can indulge no longer! We will feast with the finest foods money can buy, and then we are off to the baseball game!", Doug yelled as he made yet another balsamic house salad. Sprinkle with salt and pepper.

"Seafood feasts, my man? I'll tell you what. If you want to feast on seafood, we ought to book a flight to Seattle. I tell you now, my friend, the sushi in Seattle is better than the sushi in Tokyo. Not that I've ever been to Tokyo, but I don't see how it would be possible to have better seafood than Seattle. All the fresh fish flesh coming straight down the coast from Alaska, the Pacific has so many delicious treats to eat, we could stuff ourselves for a week and not be the least bit exasperated. They have baseball in Seattle, too. And beer. A feast, gentlemen. An old fashioned feast we shall have in Seattle, accentuated with the joy of baseball", Scott envisioned as he glazed a grilled salmon portion with reduction sauce emulsified with mustard.

"You guys are going to Seattle on Wednesday? Isn't that a bit of a stretch? They have good sushi in Boston, you know. And Boston is a lot closer. Do you even have enough money to feast in Seattle? Do you know anyone there?", Simone asked as she dusted a chocolate mousse cake with white chocolate flakes.

"Ok, maybe we won't go to Seattle. It is a bit far and expensive, especially when Boston is in our backyard. We can get chowder and calamari before the game at Cujol's on Beacon Street, the best calamari and crab cakes in Boston. You want to go? Hey Ebbi, you ever been to Cujol's on Beacon Street?", as Scott retreated his earlier proposition of a 3,000 mile trip westward.

"I make my own calamari. I rarely go out to restaurants to eat, only when I am invited and I don't want to be rude. I don't care much for restaurant food, it lacks a flavor that cannot be replicated outside the home", Ebbi replied amidst a blast of heat from the open oven door.

"You make your own? But Cujol's is the best! They make it with just the right amount of salt, and the perfect aioli sauce for dipping the large rings of fresh squid. It doesn't get any better than that my friend, the very best food money can buy", as Kendra flipped six filet mignons. Medium, medium, medium rare, well, medium rare, rare. Dust with salt and pepper.

"They probably don't use fresh squid like the kind I get from Lulu's seafood down the road, they probably use frozen product. And I doubt they use fresh olive oil for every batch of calamari they fry. They don't use sea salt, and they can't make the spicy tomato salsa I make using the fresh organic handpicked garden raised tomatoes and herbs from my garden. I doubt it is the best, but I do not doubt it is the best money can buy", came the gentle but confident reply of Ebbi.

"I always wanted to hide from my sisters, if only to avoid the embarrassment of them exposing who I really am. I don't want to give them insight into my vulnerabilities, if only to prevent them from a source of dominance over me", as Wendy stopped her work to finish her thought.

"When did you first expose your vulnerabilities to them? And why was it so painful?", inquired the chef as he knew to be delicately precise with Wendy.

"Who wants to cook in their own house? The stress, hassle, and cleanup afterwards isn't worth the time. Money is to be spent for a reason, to make our lives easier by taking advantage of the services society provides. Cujol's is a fine restaurant with excellent food, and if they're out serving the public, there is no need for people to continue cooking at home. That's how society works, and that's how we live our lives. We live in a service economy, privileged enough to have others perform the labor we would rather not perform. When people like you stay home and cook food in their homes, our economy suffers", Scott said as he took the carrots out of the steamer. Drizzle with honey.

"So we should all take a trip to Seattle, because spending more money will benefit our economy even though it will make us poor?

How does being poor help the economy? How does eating sushi in Seattle become more patriotic than eating sushi in Boston?", Kendra annunciated with a smile of sarcasm on her face.

"No, I guess not. Seattle would be a bit too excessive. But indulging in the services of the economy is more beneficial to our nation than being financial hermits. Picking my own tomatoes may be fun, but it does nothing for the American cause. The American cause is about being interconnected and contributing to the larger entity greater than the individual", Scott directly said in Ebbi's direction.

"Lulu's Seafood doesn't think I am a financial hermit. They very much appreciate my business. Who's to say I don't support and help the American economy? There is something to be said for self-sufficiency and representing one's own labor. Who's to say we have to be an exclusive service economy? Why does someone else have to represent the labor of our tasks for labor to be legitimate?", Ebbi replied as he placed three more haddock portions into the pre-heated sauté pan, onion crust side down. Dust with salt and pepper.

Robert now spoke from across the kitchen, "I always cook my own food, I don't like what the restaurants serve here in the United States. Such a bland, sweet and salty mixture to the food your culture enjoys. At home I eat jerk chicken from my grandmother's home, and prepare all food in my own kitchen to make sure the spices are just right. Never separate the artist from his paintbrush, always take pride in painting your own picture." Robert spoke in his thick Jamaican accent as he moved toward Ebbi to pick up the tub of used sauté pans from his station.

"Do you make your own ackee at home?", Ebbi asked as Robert bent over to complete his task.

"Oh yes, my very own ackee. They make good ackee at the restaurants in Jamaica, but I like to make it on my own stove top. I learned the recipe from my grandmother, and it is the best ackee your mouth will experience", Robert replied with a thick smile on his face.

"Can you teach me how to make it", Ebbi asked as he smiled and rolled his eyes to the back of his head when describing his affinity for ackee.

"Why do you need to learn the recipe for ackee? There is a Jamaican grill stand about 10 minutes from here in York, and they make the best ackee money can buy. You don't need to bother with the trouble of preparing it when someone else is willing to do it for you. Go ahead, allow yourself to enjoy the services others are willing to perform for financial compensation here in America." Kendra interrupted midway between four burger flips and cheese melting on a chicken sandwich.

Robert and Ebbi both looked at each other in amazement. Sure, they both knew the Jamaican grill stand in York, but they also understood the insightful reasons of expressing the culinary artist within. When food is cooked to its potential inside the home, there is no rival to compete with its virtue. Home cooked meals contain a metaphor impossible to achieve in the service economy. There is a passion which cannot be found when the paintbrush has been removed from the artist's hand. Ebbi prefers the virtue of his own cooking to any flavor produced by the most passionate of professional cooks in the food service industry. Ebbi likes to hold his own paintbrush.

Wendy continued her story of her sisters as she arranged the garnishing lettuce on the smoked sturgeon tray. She seemed more sullen and introspective as she ripped the lettuce leaves into perfect wavy borders.

"My sisters convinced me my mother's facial cream was in fact the invisible cream I had always dreamed of having. I remember seeing Bugs Bunny smear invisible cream on himself once, and thought this potion would be a wonderful thing to have. Being a little girl can be quite stressful, and having invisibility would be as euphoric a gift any child could ask for", Wendy continued as she started slicing the finger-sized sandwiches to be served next to the smoked sturgeon in the green room.

Chef Gregg responded, "Invisible cream, huh? I could use some of that myself from time to time. Sometimes I wish cartoons could be real. I have to talk with so many people I would rather not, salespeople who come in the service door selling products I have no intention of purchasing. Boy, if I had some invisible cream to escape their shadow when they come knockin', I'd be a happy man. Who was Bugs Bunny's product purveyor? Acme? So how did the invisible cream work for you?", Gregg helped Wendy cut and arrange the finger-sized sandwiches.

"Very funny. I'm being serious. I was a little girl and believed my older sisters. I wanted to believe it, and I didn't think my sisters would lie to me. I trusted them to tell me the truth", as Wendy's long face cringed as she remembers this ordeal involving her two older sisters.

Doug shouted from across the kitchen, "Are we still going to the Red Sox game? I don't even care about the food anymore, I just want to see some baseball. As long as we have enough beer to go around, I can sacrifice the seafood feast. I just want to be in Boston." Doug responded as he made yet another four balsamic house salads. Garnish with carrot peel.

"We could also get a barbeque pork sandwich at a place on Commonwealth Avenue I know. The most tender strips of meat money can buy, the most delectable tangy barbeque sauce your tongue has ever had the pleasure to know. A highlight destination for any trip into Boston. Ebbi, you don't eat pork either, do you?", Scott asked as he placed a chive flower garnish on the last plate of an order.

"No, I don't. I don't eat animals that walk. Only ones that swim or fly", Ebbi replied as he asked Scott to repeat the ticket order he just shouted.

"You don't eat at restaurants, you don't eat dairy, and you don't eat beef or pork? How do you survive? You've just eliminated 75% of the American diet! I would be an emaciated mess if I lived your lifestyle for more than two hours at a time", Doug stated with a high pitched inflection of his voice.

"He doesn't eat high fructose corn syrup or partially hydrogenated vegetable oil, either", Simone added as she fired up a torch for the crème brûlée. Dust with sugar, garnish with blueberries.

Doug's head was shaking as he threw salt on a salad, "make that 99%. A complete emaciated mess I would be. How is it possible to live a decent and productive happy life without enjoying the pleasures of beef, dairy, pork, high fructose corn syrup, partially hydrogenated vegetable oil, and the service of restaurants? What kind of American are you?" Doug inquired again of Ebbi's perplexing answers.

"I don't torture my digestive tract with cheese, I don't enjoy the taste of beef, I won't indulge in the flesh of pig, and I won't give in to the destructive nature of corn syrup. I spend time at home, I garden and cook meals in my own kitchen. I live with a big smile on my face, a belly's worth of nutrition in my gut, and all the future potential my spirit may embellish in", Ebbi confidently acknowledged the inquiry of Doug, answering his question in a most sincere way.

"Well, I enjoy a life quite different from you. I wouldn't want to struggle with dietary restrictions, I would rather live a life free to eat whatever I choose for my ingestion. I love my beef, dairy, pork, and service industry. In fact, I live for it. Let's all take a trip to Texas, Wisconsin, North Carolina, and New York City! Beef, dairy, pork, and service for all! Well, except for Ebbi. He can't come because he would starve to death. Traveling doesn't really seem like his thing, but we'll bring back photographs for him to look at", Doug responded with sarcastic laughter.

"Actually, I've been to all fifty states", Ebbi annunciated to the entire kitchen staff as he fired two lamb racks, one medium and one medium well. Rub with rosemary and coriander.

Wendy continued with her story, "they told me the invisible cream was real, and I rubbed it all over myself from head to toe. My sisters played along with the joke, asking each other 'where's Wendy'? At first I couldn't believe it really worked, that my fantasy had come true. For the next several hours my sisters completely ignored me. I jumped, shouted, and crawled around them, but they would not acknowledge me. I did all I could to get their attention, but they would not see me. The world had finally turned around to favor this little girl who yearned to be the little girl she wanted to be, the invisible cream worked." Wendy now had a smile on her face as she further described the story to Gregg.

"And what did you do with the invisible cream? Did you rob a bank? Spy on the neighbors? Put the cream on your parent's automobile and drive it around town?", Gregg was enthusiastic fot the reply, excited to know what a child would do if invisible powers were obtained.

"No, I ripped off all my clothes and began to dance around the house", Wendy admitted with a smirk.

"So what happened after you ripped your clothes off and started to dance around the house?", inquired Gregg of Wendy's unfinished childhood story.

"I danced and pranced my way around the house, feeling as free and alive as I had ever felt before. The wind swirled beneath my feet, the walls became a springboard for my glorious leaps into the air. I felt the freedom I had always dreamed of, dancing with every inch of my body exposed to the world, not able to hide anything or be anyone other than myself. I was me, and I sang my song as free as could be, proving to everyone who could hear my gleeful voice, my dreams had come true", Wendy stopped filling the deviled eggs when she got to this point in her story.

"I love the traffic and congestion. There's something about the pollution of a large city inspiring me to breath a little deeper and inhale the ambiance of a thriving city, full of people, trade, and conversation. The grit, the smoke, the rats scurrying through the park. City energy breathes life into all crevices of its precinct, making significant what was once predictable. The culture of Boston is enough to put a smile on my face and a confession of love on my lips for the capital city of New England. Never would I commit any crimes or atrocities toward our city or its people, if only for my reverence and loyalty to its culture, past history, and future potential. No person could commit crimes against a city they love as dearly as I love Boston, no person could commit atrocities towards a passion they hold dear", Scott confessed as he laid down another seven plates in preparation for the finished food orders coming from Ebbi and Kendra.

"My sisters continued to ignore my magnificent dancing and singing, allowing me to become more convinced of the invisible cream's success. How they held back from laughter at my naive gullibility I will never know. The humor must have been overwhelming for them. But there I was, dancing and singing in front of them, completely nude and completely ignorant of reality", as Wendy began filling the deviled eggs again, dusting them with paprika.

"To love a city is to love one's family. Cities need to cultivate their citizen's love, to ensure the city will realize its future potential", Scott continued amidst a sea of food orders streaming into the kitchen.

"Are you from the city of Boston, Scott", came an inquiry from Kendra.

"No, but close. Revere, Massachusetts. I went into Boston every chance I got while growing up. The city's lure could never keep me away for too many moments at a time. Revere is a great place for a child to grow up ... well, usually. Times could be tough in Revere, but culture was always relevant, and I am thankful for that. I don't think I could ever live in Revere again, if only because I couldn't take the strain of living so close to a city. Now that I'm in Maine, I can't live away from the beach", Scott replied as he coordinated the last wave of orders coming back to the kitchen. Garnish with scallion threads.

Kendra cut in, "it's funny how priorities change throughout life. When I was a child I couldn't live without fried chicken strips, but now I can't even lick them with my tongue. The taste is repugnant to my palate, let alone the sauces served with them at fast food restaurants to disguise their awful flavor. Whatever happened to fresh chicken meat and homemade stock? Orange marmalade and toasted sesame seeds?" Kendra asked as she flipped yet another three filet mignons. Medium rare, medium rare, medium rare. Brush with olive oil.

Wendy continued, "little did I realize the falsity of invisible cream, flaunting my small body all over the house in an embarrassing display of immature trust for elder siblings. I remember this moment and wince at my stupidity, wishing I could reverse time to stop myself. I danced and sang for quite a long while, pleasing my sisters because they had found a way to preoccupy me without requiring their attention", Wendy continued before placing kale around the far borders of the banquet tray.

"They didn't stop you from dancing? They allowed you to continue even though they knew it would be devastating once you uncovered the reality of the situation?", Gregg tried to help a sullen Wendy before placing the cherry tomatoes atop the kale leaves.

"I used to eat blue ice pops, the kind that would stain my teeth and make me a blue monster for at least three days at a time. My mother would get angry at me, but being a blue monster is great for scaring the dog", Doug added before mixing a caesar salad, extra anchovies hold the croutons.

Ebbi responded, "my mother used to make homemade granola, and we used to eat it as a snack. It wasn't colored with blue paint, but it did taste wonderful. The nutrition in the granola far exceeded any scientific measuring device or food service label." Nobody could understand what Ebbi was really talking about, as they had not had mothers so dedicated to the health of their stomachs.

Wendy continued further, "the insight they exposed makes me squirm with a discomforting insecurity, because their insight was used for my humiliating demise to last a lifetime", Wendy responded before lifting her finished tray onto the rack.

Kendra added a story about her own mother, "my mother used to take us out to dinner on our birthdays, showing us a good time on special occasions. We always begged and pleaded with her to spend more money than she would initially invest in our enjoyment, always wanting more out than what she provided. When it was her turn to watch us, she would always treat us to a movie and ice cream. We would always try to talk her into one more movie, one more ice cream, or one more toy from the store. Sometimes it worked, most of the time she got angry with our insatiable appetite for her time and money." Kendra removed six filet mignons from the grill, placing them on serving plates.

"Your parents were divorced?", Doug inquired without hesitation. Spinach salad, hold the bacon.

"Yes. Since the time I was three years old. We always got angry at our father for not spending money on our entertainment like mother did. He always wanted to stay home and spend time with us without the distractions of movies and ice cream stores. Looking back, we had a much more satiating relationship with our father, as he would offer time without monetary conditions", Kendra added as she reflected on her past life and foresight into the future.

"I continued to dance and sing, waving my arms and prancing my legs through the air until my parents came home. I heard them walk in the door, and I thought this to be an optimal opportunity to showcase my newfound invisible power. Wendy was now Wendy, invisible but free, with all future potential ahead to fulfill spiritual satiation. I danced down the stairs to greet my parents, confidently assured they could not see me", Wendy continued as she stopped her work, concentrating on this moment of childhood etched into her brain.

Scott now spoke of his parents to Kendra, hoping she may understand something about him. "My parents always took us to the toy store when they needed to calm us down from hyperactivity and sullen depression. We would beg and plead with them to take us, even when they didn't want to, if only to use the toy store as a symbol of their love. Anything was better than being around our house. My siblings and I would beg incessantly until my father conceded to take us to the toy store, and a restaurant serving processed beef and cheese to follow. I could not relate to anything in our home or our family's values, but I could relate to everything in the store. I became emotionally attached to toys and processed beef because they were the symbols of my parent's love", Scott explained the plight of his childhood as well as his affection for beef and dairy food.

"I danced my heart out in front of my parents, waiting for my invisible powers to be confirmed, proving I could now be myself without fear of critical judgment. Being able to express independence in my own home was a treasure filling my head with wonderful enlightenment and confidence for future potential. The world finally seemed friendly to me, warm and encouraging to the satiation of my spirit. It's an encouragement I had never felt before, and one I was thrilled to pursue. I danced and sang with the passion of eternity", Wendy lamented through her crab puff arrangement.

"How long did it last", Gregg inquired with ardent intrigue.

"It didn't. My world of future potential came to a sudden halt when my father looked at me in the eye and said: "Wendy, put some clothes on.""

Sleepless Nights and Liquid Food

"One thing to know about me is that I'm a very bottom line kind of guy. I don't care about what you can say about anything else, because when it comes down to it, I'm all about the money. You can run around all day thinking about this and preaching about that, but if the money isn't there, you're finished. Done. Terminated. Money controls everything, because if you don't have it, you're nothing", Tyson spoke to Wallace as he sliced lemons into wedges. Both are bartenders at the Homestead Restaurant, and both are very dedicated to their jobs.

Tyson prepares his bar by stocking wines, beer, liquor, and garnishes for cocktail drinks. Alcohol is Tyson's business, service his craft. People come to his bar, not just to whet their palates with alcoholic refreshments, but to have their food and beverages prepared and served to them by professionals. Leaving the work of cleaning dirty dishes to others. This is why people come to restaurants, and these are the services Tyson performs. Tyson is also an entertainer, talking to people and socializing in a professional way.

"Money is very important", Wallace said as he flipped another page of his newspaper. He did not listen with much enthusiasm. Wallace is not scheduled to begin work for another 25 minutes, arriving at work early to drink coffee and read the newspaper before the onslaught of labor begins. He sits at the bar, glancing occasionally at the clock to assure his slow lull has not overstepped its bounds. Without much desire to excel in the art of bartending, Wallace slowly sips his coffee and reads the newspaper.

Wallace takes little else from his job besides the money. He doesn't like people much, as they always ask the same questions, tell the same jokes, and talk about the weather. He does not much care for the sacrifices his body must endure for the job, either. Falling asleep at 4 in the morning, rotten fingernails, an ulcer, and alcoholism top the list of ailments suffered from bartending. Not that he has to be an alcoholic, but being surrounded by so much temptation makes it difficult to remain disciplined.

Tyson began speaking again as he stocked cranberry juice. "You can go around saying higher food quality tastes better, but at the end of the day, what does it mean for the bottom line? What does it mean for the finances of a restaurant? I don't care what something tastes like, or if it was grown and picked in your backyard, it's our business to give the customer what they want and charge them as much as we can. Most people can't tell the difference between an organic carrot and a conventional one, so what's the point of serving organic? Why is it worth the hassle? Profit maximization is not found in organic produce." Tyson was referring to a previous conversation he had with Ebbi about food quality and passions.

The conversation paused as Tyson left to grab some limes from the back. Wallace sat at the bar, reading his newspaper and sipping coffee, trying not to think about stress and politics. The time spent setting up a bar can be an interesting time in a bartender's life. It is an ideal time to think without pressure. Much needs to be done before the opening of service, preparing for every drink a customer may order. Limes, orange slices, lemons, olives … the list goes on and on. It can be a grueling ordeal, but bartenders find a way to make it work five or six nights a week. And they still find time to enjoy a snack, drink, or cigarette when the mood is just right.

Wallace wakes up less than an hour before his shift begins because of his late night schedule. The nocturnal schedule is fun and lively, but can become a detriment to health for young people like Wallace. Intoxicants are abound, promiscuous sex is common, and sleep is not a priority. The money he makes does not stay in his pocket for long. Battling omnipresent insomnia, Wallace will drink himself to sleep at the expense of his liver. Sobriety is too painful, like opening the window shades too quickly after waking from dark sleep. Sleep and food are seen as inconveniences of life, which makes it a good thing Wallace doesn't eat or sleep very much. Most of his nutritional intake is done through alcohol, his taste buds have been destroyed by cigarettes, and his dreams are infested with nightmares.

"Time isn't worth anything if it is not financially productive. Most people wouldn't be able to tell the difference between homemade mustard and a processed mustard product, and in all actuality, most customers would prefer the processed product. Ebbi is back there telling me how great his homemade mustard is, and how great it would be to bring his mustard into the restaurant to serve. Do you really think people would want it? Do you think they would care? Do you think they could tell the difference? Between extra labor hours and ingredients needed to make the mustard, we actually save money buying mustard product from purveyors. No hassle, just the mustard people want to eat. Opening a jar and spooning the mustard is a lot easier than making it from scratch", as Tyson cut the limes into wedges. He wears rubber gloves because lime juice is known to ignite searing pain when fingers are riddled with little cuts and bloody nicks. With so many cuts on his fingers, Tyson uses protection to assure himself the comfort he deserves when cutting citrus fruit.

"I thrive on consistency", Wallace apathetically replied as his attention remained focused on the newspaper. Not wanting to be bothered with the banter of work or the conflicting ideologies of Tyson and Ebbi, Wallace kept to his newspaper and steaming coffee. Originally an intelligent young man, the bartending business has sucked the intelligence straight from his brain. Intoxicated minds tend to lose their wits when not used in an intelligent sort of way. Wallace likes to keep himself informed of the news and new ideas if only to convince himself he has not lost the wits he knows he has lost.

Turning first to the sports page before the comics and crossword, he eventually reads the editorials for the informative insight he longs to have. He reads the comics slowly to avoid an eminent arrival at the editorials. He likes the editorials, but since they are more challenging and time consuming to his mind, he would rather skip them if not for his guilty conscious. A mind is a terrible thing to waste, and he wouldn't want to cause such injury to his mother. If it wasn't for his insecurity, guilt, and maternal loyalty he would spend more time on the comics.

Tyson continued, assuming Wallace was still listening. "I need to give people the consistency and familiar service they expect. That's my job. That's what I am here for. I'm not here to be a maverick of heresy, I'm here to provide a service in exchange for money. If I wasn't able to provide these products and services, people would not want to spend their money here, and I would be out of a job. The art of making money is not providing the best quality product, it is providing consistency and familiarity to assure the customer's return to spend their money once again. Creating an addiction is the name of the business game, it's what separates failure from success in the world of financial business", Tyson exclaimed to an otherwise distracted Wallace as he finished cutting the limes. Next he would portion out the maraschino cherries, another task requiring rubber gloves, except not for pain avoidance, but to elude the red paint stain these cherries inflict upon the skin.

Tyson is the bar manager at the Homestead, and takes his position very seriously. Partaking in all business relative to the restaurant, he considers the Homestead to be his home. As he would. Tyson spends nearly 80 hours a week at the Homestead, making the Homestead home to Tyson. Be that as it may, many of those 80 hours are not spent laboring. Tyson spends much of his free time at the Homestead doing many non-labor related activities. Creating gossip feuds amongst coworkers, he thrives on the dramatic element injected into relationship dynamics. Chatting with customers, cigarette breaks, and getting into mischief takes up most of the 80 hours he spends here.

Tyson drinks before the shift, gambles after the shift, and becomes obsessively preoccupied with little odd jobs around the restaurant. The Homestead is his surrogate home, providing food and drink, bathroom and bedroom, shelter and emotional connection. He sporadically eats the finger food available from the kitchen, drinks copious amounts of liquor behind the bar, uses the bathroom frequently, has been known to sleep here on many occasions when walking home is too much of a challenge, spends rainy days watching rain from the Homestead window, and connects Homestead workers to the family he never had. Or does have. He quarrels and creates conflicts with nearly every worker at the Homestead, and is never happy unless he is at odds with everyone who works here. He has a selected few people with whom he gets along with, and none of them are single men. Being single himself and dating promiscuously, he is very insecure about other single men who could create competition for the promiscuous women he pursues. He needs the identity of being the only man available for single ladies, and hence, prefers to associate with male friends who are in committed relationships and do not threaten his competitive nature.

Wallace spoke up from behind his newspaper, answering in a way which may or may not have demonstrated to Tyson that he was paying attention. "As long as they tip well, I couldn't care less. I don't care whether the Homestead is able to produce its profit margins or not. I'm just interested in making the money I make for myself every night. I want my time to be worth the effort. This restaurant means nothing more to me than a place to make money. If the Homestead were to fail, I'd go out and find myself another bartending job without thinking twice about it", as Wallace sat back and continued to read his paper.

Wallace still has 20 minutes left until his shift begins, and has every intention of using these last moments for all they are worth. He will not get to sleep tonight until sunrise, repeating the same routine again tomorrow. Reaffirming his intelligence through the newspaper. Tyson took Wallace's comments to mean he was paying attention, which may or may not have been true. Either way, Tyson saw this as an opportunity to further the conversation.

"The object is to get customers addicted to your service. If they become addicted, they will return to satiate their desires. The trick is to quench their addiction without satiating their desires. The question is, how do we get people addicted? How do we quench without satiating? The answer is simple. Provide familiar and consistent services, as well as the food they enjoy. You can't tell people what they want to eat, you have to open choices to the most popular demands. Who wants to satiate? If we satiate, we lose addiction. And if we lose addiction, we lose profit expansion. Screw homemade mustard. Screw passions. Passions only get in the way of dollars.

This is the most basic and fundamental concept of a capitalist society, to take a product and expand its profitability", Tyson said as he stacked wine glasses.

A person of debauchery, Tyson cultivates ingenuity when it comes to the business of money profits. The alcohol, drugs, and excessive ejaculations has not intoxicated his mind away from the ideals of a capitalist political economy. Not always the most honest and admirable man of ethics, Tyson is successful in his own defined ways. Ends always justify the means. His ideals will probably not hold up to health and longevity, even though they will succeed in short-term gratification. Even though contradiction's destiny is to be exposed for its fallacies, Tyson moves forward with no apology for self-proclaimed prophecy.

Tyson finished his glass stacking tasks and brought out three large empty jars. The jars are used to make fruitinis, a fruit punch made by marinating fresh fruit in vodka for a period of several days inside a jar. An easy concoction to make, it is one of the most popular drinks the bar offers as well as the most expensive. The largest amount of labor expended on the fruitini is the fruit cutting required for its preparation. This usually does not take Tyson long to do. He had already cut the fruit for the frutini, and pulls out a container holding the fresh cut kiwis and strawberries. He begins to pour vodka into the jar, giving the fruity refreshment its alcoholic kick. Just as he started to pour in the first bottle of vodka, Kendra walked out from the kitchen to pour herself a glass of water.

"Making fruitinis, huh?", Kendra asked as her water trickled out from the spout and into her glass.

"That's the idea. People love these things. Give people something they like and they come back for more. That's the name of the game", Tyson replied as he watched the glugging of vodka spill its way into the jar.

"I thought I heard you tell a customer the other night we use a higher quality brand of vodka for the fruitinis? The vodka you're using is terrible and cheap. Are you aware of this mistake?", Kendra pointed out as her cup became full of water.

"Wallace, did you order any more rum from the distributor? We were low yesterday and I forgot to do it this morning. And where did you put the cocktail olives?", as Tyson avoided the question Kendra raised in an effort to hide dishonesty. He tells customers the fruitinis are made with a higher quality vodka than they really are, to boost their appeal and the price tag. What the people don't know won't hurt them, anyway. At least until, of course, contradiction is exposed for its fallacious foundations.

Kendra took her cue and headed back to the kitchen with her glass of water. She was reminded yet again of why she does not want to work outside the kitchen. The level of required dishonesty would be too much conflict for her to handle. Pay is lower in the kitchen, but the personal values preserved are worth the lost money. Kendra prefers the honest hard work of food preparation at the Homestead, without the pomp of service with a fake smile. She laughs to herself as she makes her way back to the kitchen, knowing she caught Tyson in another lie he will not want to discuss in his gossip riddled conversations. Above all else, integrity and honesty are critical values for a person to attach on their name, especially for a bartender who relies on the confidence of his customers to return their business time and time again. Tyson cannot be exposed for the dishonesty he is prone to providing his customers with. To do so would be disastrous for his career path, disastrous for his foundation of ideology.

Tyson struggles with the face of integrity so crucial for bottom line ideology to be successful. The two very often collide and conflict with one another. Substituting lesser quality vodka when higher quality vodka is spoken of is only the tip of a very large and cold iceberg. Tyson has also been known to put extra drink orders on a customer's tab when he feels they are too intoxicated to notice the disparity. Tyson has also been known to cheat the Homestead, not recording certain drink orders and placing the money from the sale into his own pocket without remorse. Maximizing profits and maintaining integrity can be quite a challenging simultaneous duality to maintain amidst looming ethics and the difficulty of remaining disciplined surrounded by omnipresent temptation.

"Did you see that man in here the other night, with funny glasses and big gums, holding onto the heavy-set woman with a curly afro? Did I tell you what he said to me before he left the bar?",

Tyson asked Wallace during his restocking of rum and gin. Wallace looked up to hear the gossip. Gossip can be quite entertaining, and it sparked Wallace's attention away from the newspaper.

"No, what did he say to you? Wasn't he the one who kept looking at you like he wanted to punch you in the face? Man, that guy had some big gums", Wallace responded as he sipped his coffee while sucking in a breath of air.

"Yeah, he was staring at me the whole night because he thought I was staring at him. I really just couldn't get over his gums. I couldn't believe how big they were, and how small his teeth were. Remember how I said he needed to have some plastic surgery?", Tyson chuckled as he swung a bottle of gin into its place on the shelf behind him.

"Yeah, I couldn't get over them myself. Such small teeth. What did he say before he left? Did he punch you in the face for staring at his gums?", Wallace now put down his newspaper to provide his undivided attention to the end of the story. The stories that develop in the restaurant business are what keep many of the employees from leaving. Being a part of the stories, and listening to them from co-workers is the most exciting part of the job. So many different people come in the restaurant every night, and there is an interesting story behind most, and something to be said about all.

"I guess he thought I was coming on to him in a sexual way or something, because as he was leaving, he said he likes being one of the boys. That he likes to hang out at the beach after the bars close down, near the volleyball courts. He gave me his contact information and said we need to spend some time together. I told him I wasn't gay, but I was flattered, and he better stick to the girlfriend he came in with. He ain't pretty enough to get anyone else. He said she was boring, and I was the cutest thing he had ever seen. He licked his finger, patted my hand, and walked out the door", Tyson chuckled to himself. It is always flattering to know someone thinks you are attractive, even when the attraction is not reciprocated.

"I'd just take what I could get. Those gums are brutal. Even if his woman has a curly afro, I wouldn't do anything to mess that up", Wallace spoke as he took another sip of coffee and continued reading his newspaper. This gossip was good, but not stellar. He was slowly making his way to the editorial section, although he procrastinated his arrival with subtle reluctance. Reading comics and doing an easy crossword is much preferable to the thinking of philosophical issues and political debates in the editorials. Wallace will eventually get to it, if only to satisfy his own desire to make vein attempts at stimulating his intoxicated mind with intellect.

"I'll tell you something, if I had big gums or any facial deformity, I would get the plastic surgery. How ever much money it costs, let medical science take care of it. People can be so ignorant, so destructive to themselves. That's why people with lots of money are happier and live longer than poor people. They have the ability to access medical science and technology", Tyson said as he leans on the bar to sip his coffee near to Wallace. Tyson likes to talk just for the sake of talking, even if his words fall upon deaf ears. Wallace is still very infatuated with his newspaper, making sure Tyson's words fall on deaf ears. Talking is just another part of the job Wallace can do without. He hardly even looks up as Tyson leans next to him.

"Money is good. It can do a lot of things for you. Think we will make much of it tonight?", Wallace asked as he looked over the comics one last time. His coffee was almost gone, but he knew his presence at work was not crucially imperative because of the relaxed attitude Tyson leans against the bar with.

"Good thing I never needed any plastic surgery. I was blessed with a fantastic looking face without any need of fixing. I am the model medical science designs their craft around. Women fall in love with me just the way I am", Tyson smugly said as he sipped his coffee and chuckled to himself.

"Don't you use erection enhancing pills?", Wallace cut into Tyson's wonderful depiction of himself with unyielding dry witty sarcasm.

"Who doesn't? I give women what they want, and if I need some help from a few small pills, I will take advantage of my resources. It doesn't make me a bad person, it makes me a resourceful man. I give women the privilege of my erection, and if I can give them more, I will do it for them", Tyson reaffirmed his self image against the onslaught of dry witty sarcasm he faced from an apathetic Wallace. Tyson will do anything to convince people of his honesty and integrity, even if it means lying and being dishonest.

Wallace didn't really know how to respond, or if he really wanted to. He just wanted Tyson to leave him alone. The argument would be too overwhelming for him to finish, and disruptive of his coffee and newspaper. Wallace knew about the crimes of dishonesty Tyson was prone to, often taking part in them himself. It's all about the money, and as long as it doesn't hurt anyone, Wallace is willing to participate. He understands the issues at hand and their immediate consequences, but doesn't care as long as his pocket is full and his rap sheet clear. He uses erection enhancing pills himself.

As Wallace flips the newspaper over towards the editorial section, he sees an advertisement. He pauses to read. It says:

Salted Refreshments

Pasty mouth, Wipe the brow
Salted water within, All water without.
Tongue parched, Eyes dry
Salted water within, All water without.

Dehydration abound
Salted water within, All water without.
Must drink
Salted water within, All water without.
Thirsty from
Salted water within.
Thirsty from
All water without.

Quenching thirst,
Salted water within.
Quenching thirst,
All water without.

Thirsty from quenching thirst,
Salted water within.
All water without.
Quenching thirst with thirsty,
Salted Refreshments.

The advertisement made Wallace ponder for a moment. The addictive nature of American products only makes people more thirsty to buy more products. Quenching without satiating. The eternal thirst of addiction, the cycle of ingesting salted refreshments. At least DAFA is trying to do good things. But Wallace is too infatuated with his coffee and newspaper to discuss and ponder these issues. He flips to the editorial section to relieve his angst of guilt, reading the first editorial to catch his attention.

Newspaper Clippings
(Editorial Section)

<u>Harvesting Youth Addictions</u>
Editorial by Nelson Jouster

It is with great concern we turn our attention to children and the ugly head of profit margins violating our innocent youth. No longer can we view marketing motives of large corporations as a just way to increase revenues for stockholders and corporate interests alike. Because when these types of motives seek to infiltrate and violate our children through the harvesting of youth addictions, they cease to be justified. As a nation, and a culture, we cannot afford to let violating injustices be an accepted condition of our society. Interests far greater than profit margins and marketing strategies depend on our resistance to harvesting youth addictions. These interests include physical and mental health, freedom from addictive dependence and debt, freedom for livelihood, and freedom to pursue happiness without detriments to physical and mental health, addictive dependence and debt, a stifled livelihood, or a shunned pursuit of happiness.

When persons are subject to the dependence of addiction, freedom is exchanged for their health. Persons under addiction are willing

to reorganize their schedules and routines,
friendships and livelihoods to ensure their
access to a particular addictive agent.
Freedom becomes a weaker concern as physical
and mental health become weaker concerns.
Irrational decision making begins to
infiltrate the mind.

Superior marketing strategists know this
pattern of addicted dependence all too well.
Although it is within ethical marketing
strategies to pursue addiction dependence
under capitalist political economy, no ethical
code has ever stated, either implicitly or
contextually, that perpetrating addictions to
children is ever justified. It is now that
superior marketing strategists ought to be
brought to justice for their crimes against
children.

The addictive vice spoken of today is
caffeine. Highly addictive and highly
marketed to children, caffeine has become our
era's socially accepted addictive drug. In
yesterday's society nicotine was the socially
accepted addictive drug, in last week's
society it was cocaine. Tomorrow it will be
any number of vices society will accept when
profit margins outweigh the health of our
citizens. It is with great outrage and
disgust that these ethics are practiced in
America. It is with outrage and disgust that
American corporations be called into greater
social responsibility for the dispersal of
poisonous products.

At present time, caffeine has not been
determined through legitimate proof to be an
addictive drug. This comes as no surprise to
common sense, since superior marketing
strategists work to suppress legitimate proof
from becoming common knowledge. Legitimate
proof is malleable enough to influence any

government politician, scientific researcher, or marketing strategist; malleable enough to make truth what they wish it to be without the guide of common sense.

Common sense tells us caffeine, and all its forms, is an unsafe addictive drug for our children to ingest. Caffeine is an addictive drug. Common sense proves this point beyond all reasonable doubt. When a friend reveals they are subject to a searing headache unless a caffeine addiction is sufficiently satiated by a certain hour of the morning, caffeine is addictive. When a friend reveals they are willing to go many steps out of their way to obtain a caffeine vice, caffeine is addictive. When a friend reveals they are unable to produce a bowel movement without a caffeine vice, caffeine is addictive. When a friend reveals they cannot live through a day without a certain number of caffeine vices, caffeine is addictive. When a friend reveals they have a complete absence of social personality without a sufficient amount of caffeine vice, caffeine is addictive. Alas, when you yourself realize the power of caffeine amongst social settings, and the power caffeine has to control and alter plans and moods, personalities and motivations of people around you, caffeine is addictive.

It is with educated predictions that caffeine will be recognized as an addictive, controlled, and possibly illegal, narcotic drug in the future. To laugh or balk at this notion is to be unwise. In the 1920's, cocaine was not thought to be a threatening substance, commonplace in society, and not worthy of narcotic recognition. In fact, cocaine was thought to be an ethical ingredient in soft drink products marketed to children. The commonplace of cocaine as an ingredient made the superior marketing

strategy of cocaine-laced soft drinks ethical
for its time.

Over time, people began to realize cocaine's
addictive nature as common sense began to
supercede legitimate proof. Discovered were
many of its addictive dependent
characteristics, along with many physical and
emotional side affects injurious to future
potential. Eventually, it became an illegal
narcotic, certainly not suitable for children.

The second historical American example of
socially accepted addictive drugs is nicotine.
Immediately following World War II, many
soldiers came home from military service as
addicted smokers. Legitimate proof did not
consider nicotine to be an addictive drug, and
was frequently perpetrated to American youth
with the superior marketing strategies of
large corporations. The superior marketing
strategy of nicotine corporations made
addicted smokers out of children, creating
addicted smokers for many loyal decades to
come. A lifelong addiction to nicotine
created enormous profits for corporations.

Nicotine addiction eventually became a social
dilemma as time went forth. Many adverse
long-term affects of nicotine addiction
surfaced including cancer, emphysema, and
heart disease. These long-term ramifications
left injurious scars on our societal family,
and have deterred the future potential of
several generations behind their course.

While common sense might have told us nicotine
was addictive and adverse to our health,
security, and freedom many years prior,
legitimate proof was able to keep common sense
stifled. It was not until many decades after
abundant and capricious smoking that Americans
acknowledged the damaging characteristics of

nicotine addiction. Financial disease, limits of freedom, and general impatience and irritability are affects of nicotine addiction.

Nicotine addiction was perpetrated to American youth until common sense became too obvious to hide it any longer. The consequence was a banning of nicotine vending in public schools, banning sale of nicotine to minors, banning of superior nicotine marketing strategies, and social frowning when nicotine addiction is targeted toward American youth.

It is with these historical documents that educated predictions have been made. With the use of common sense, and without the lethargy and political turmoil of legitimate proof, caffeine addiction can be acknowledged with more expeditious consciousness than its recent predecessors of cocaine and nicotine. Americans cannot afford to wait for the lethargy of legitimate proof. It is with outrage and disgust that lessons of past injuries have fallen upon deaf ears. To fathom the idea of caffeine machines in our children's schools, making caffeine addiction readily available, easy, and encouraged, would make any common sense American vomit our cultural bile. Superior marketing strategies and profit margins ought never take precedence over the health and freedom of future potential for our children.

Conjuring addictions in children is worthy of the high crime of treason against our great nation for subverting life, liberty, and the pursuit of happiness. To perpetrate lifelong addictions and addictive dependence is of the lowest decency human kind has to offer, and worthy of criminal prosecution.

The nutritional value of present-day caffeinated soft drinks consists of sugar, salt, and caffeine. Caffeinated vices are intended to do little but harvest addiction in human beings, to make sure the satiation of thirst will never find remedy as long as addictive agents are consumed. The combination of salt, sugar, and caffeine ensure the addicted will never be fully hydrated or satisfied after consumption. This is by no means a horrible mistake. The never ending thirst of a caffeine drinker is well intentioned, as it fits the superior marketing strategies of large controlling corporations.

Educated predictions say that many adverse health affects will rise in the years to come. Common sense says that addiction and dehydration can only be suppressed for a limited time by legitimate proof before common sense rises to the surface. Urinary tract infection, intestinal disease, colon disease, stomach disease, headaches and assorted brain ailments, nerve disease, blood circulation diseases, and skin irritations will be associated with caffeine addiction in the years to come.

With a historical perspective of educated predictions, citizens of America in 1950 did not realize the heart, lung, and blood diseases associated with nicotine addiction. And it is with this historical perspective that citizens of present day America cannot realize the long term affects of caffeine addiction. It has now become merely a question of whether or not we are willing to listen to our common sense, or if we can afford to wait for the lethargy of legitimate proof to slowly surface before we protect our children from the superior marketing strategies of large controlling corporations.

As a society it is our duty to provide our
children with optimal future potential for
their individual health, as well as our
collective societal health. American future
potential is rooted in the pursuit of life,
liberty, and happiness; its ideology rooted in
a life absent of debt and dependence. Living a
life free of debt and dependence is the sacred
gift we must extend to our children.

It is time to call our controlling
corporations to become more socially
responsible towards the sacred interests of
our society. No longer can we view products
of any particular corporation as mere
commodities, but as vehicles of community
interest for their relevance to American
future potential. The perpetration of
caffeine products to our children is
despicable. The superior marketing
advertisements targeting children to acquire
caffeine addiction dependency is grotesque. As
a nation, we must teach ourselves and our
children, that independence and future
potential are sacred. Public common sense
will certainly prevail over superior marketing
strategies and lethargic legitimacy, but how
long will we have to wait?

Recipe Book
"Top Secret"

Haddock

7 oz. Portion of Haddock
Onion Crust (bread crumbs consist of granulated dried bread and caramelized onions; prepared before service)
Olive Oil
Butter
Salt
Fresh Cracked Pepper

Portions of haddock are cut and stowed before service begins. Remove haddock portion from the low cooler and place on plate. Cover haddock with olive oil. Salt and pepper top side of haddock, careful not to over-salt. Press onion crust into top-side of haddock flesh, making it stick as best as it can hold. Place crusted haddock into pre-heated pan with oil/butter mixture, crust side down.

Be careful not to splatter self with hot oil/butter mixture when placing fish into pan, especially if fish is watery. When onion crust becomes brown, flip and place sauté pan into oven. Allow to cook in 400 degree oven for at least seven minutes, but no more than twelve.

Haddock is one of the most popular dishes in New England, as well as the most popular at the Homestead. The sauté cook will often piggy-back haddock orders as a necessary strategy to preserving efficiency. Piggy-backing is when the sauté cook waits to fire multiple orders of haddock all at once, instead of one order at a time.

When removing haddock from the pan for plating, gentle care is required to assure the delicate fish will not break. Haddock becomes very soft and flaky when cooked, and falls apart rather easily. If this happens, depending on the extent of the damage, another haddock will need to be fired for replacement.

If multiple haddock portions are fired it will hinder efficiency, displease the chef, and frustrate the sauté cook. Such frustration often causes the sauté cook to slam the ruined fish into a garbage can and kick the cursed pan into a wall with the loud smack. This dish is simple in its nature, but can become very monotonous and tedious with its high level of repetition and attention to delicate handling.

Serve haddock with wild mushroom risotto (prepared before service), vegetable of the night (sugar snap peas), and decorate with basil infused olive oil. Garnish with fresh chive flowers.

For tonight's service:
39 times repeated
0 returned to kitchen
3 complements
23% food cost

Filet Mignon

8 oz. Portion Filet Mignon
Olive Oil
Salt
Pepper
Demi-glace
Red Wine (in demi-glace)

Place 8 oz. portion of filet mignon immediately on grill upon order; oiling, salting, and peppering throughout the entire process. Filet mignon is pre-packaged in vacuum sealed pouches, unless the kitchen is skilled enough to butcher filets by hand. Filet mignon requires two precise grill marks on each side of the filet at acute angles, making diamonds of intersecting lines.

Acute diamond grill marks are important for presentation, but also serve as a timing reference for the grill cook. The depth and color of the mark reveals the amount of time the filet has spent on the grill. Much like a musician tapping their foot to guide a song's rhythm, grill marks guide the rhythm of a steak's temperature. Careful not to overcook. Fire, flip, turn, flip; the grill process of a filet mignon in precise metered steps.

The most important aspect of grilling steak is arriving at the specified temperature. Medium-rare is the most popular. Customers are more than willing to send back wrongfully cooked filet mignon to the kitchen. Having filet mignon sent back to the kitchen hinders efficiency, displeases the chef, and frustrates the grill cook. For these reasons, grill cooks will commonly under-cook steaks to avoid the risk of overcooking them; placing an under-cooked steak back on the grill is much easier, less costly, and less traumatic than firing a new steak if the first one is overcooked.

Overcooking a steak entails a tongue lashing from the chef for losing food cost, disappointed moans from co-workers who don't want to deal with re-plating erred entrees, and a free dessert to the table as an apology from the manager. Having filet mignon come back to the kitchen is very embarrassing for the grill cook, and constitutes a large source of stress for the position. After a filet is cooked just below its specified temperature, it must be rested off the grill for residual cooking, giving the meat a chance to re-absorb its juices and complete the cooking cycle. If the filet is not undercooked before the residual cooking phase, it will overcook by the time it reaches the table of destination.

Ladle a small portion of demi-glace over the filet after being plated for service.

Serve with garlic mashed potatoes (prepared before service), vegetable of the night (sugar snap peas), and demi-glace (prepared before service).

For tonight's service:
32 times repeated
4 sent back to kitchen
2 re-fired for overcooking
7 complements
31% food cost

Shrimp Scampi

8 Large Shrimp	**Mushrooms**
Olive Oil	**Lemon Juice**
Butter	**Green Onion**
Three-Fingers of Garlic	**Salt**
White Wine	**Pepper**

Place eight peeled and de-veined shrimp (prepared prior to service) in a preheated sauté pan of olive oil and butter mixture. After 2 minutes, throw in a handful of sliced mushrooms (sliced before service). After 3 minutes, put in three fingers of chopped garlic (chopped prior to service). After 30 seconds to caramelize garlic, de-glaze pan with white wine and allow to reduce for 1 minute. Turn off heat.

Place a tab of butter in pan and allow to melt, combining and thickening the wine reduction. Add lemon juice, adjust taste with salt and pepper. Place in scampi dish and garnish with green onions.

A very fast dish, its highest difficulty is preventing the garlic from burning. Garlic will burn very quickly if not deglazed in timely fashion.

Scampi can often be mistimed with other orders on the same ticket because its speed can be taken for granted. Scampi is fast, but can be a painful ordeal if the necessary ingredients have not been adequately prepared and stowed by the sauté cook. This dish rarely gets sent back to the kitchen, because even if an error had been made in its preparation, the cook can melt extra butter in the pan to mask the erred flavor. An easy dish for the sauté cook, and one not meeting with much difficulty or protest, except if the garlic burns or the ingredients are not sufficiently prepared and stowed.

Serve with rice pilaf (prepared before service), vegetable of the night (sugar snap peas), and garnish with a lemon wedge.

For tonight's service:

16 times repeated	0 complements
0 sent back to kitchen	20% food cost

Grilled Salmon

6 oz. portion fresh salmon fillet
Salt
Pepper
Balsamic Vinegar Reduction Emulsified with Mustard (prepared before service)

Remove salmon portion from cooler, and place on grill, service side down. Grill marks are important for presentation of salmon, but not necessary for temperature guidance. Salt and pepper immediately. Use a long spatula to flip salmon, preventing any delicate flaky collapse into the grill.

Slightly under-cook for full flavor of salmon, but be careful not to excessively undercook, because customers will send it back. Cooks and food passionates readily enjoy undercooked or raw fresh fish, but many American palates do not enjoy or trust this type of preparation.

Farm raised salmon is a fine product, but domesticated animals are not without their drawbacks. The acquisition of wild salmon is a special treat for food passionates, for its meatier, fuller, and more delicate flavor than its farmed counter-part. Tonight the Homestead serves farm-raised salmon, next week wild Chinook Salmon will be served with a reduced peach and coconut sauce as a nightly special.

Grilling salmon is somewhat of an inconvenience for the grill-cook because flipping and removing fish from the grill requires a good amount of attention. Attention is not always available to utilize at all moments of the night, and many pieces of fish have fallen to the grill's fiery depths due to this ignorance. Salmon softens as it cooks, and easily falls apart if attention is not optimal.

The greatest amount of labor expended on the salmon entree is cutting it into portions from its whole form before service. Salmon is delivered as a whole fish to the Homestead, minus the guts and scales, and the kitchen staff cleans and portions into product form. Trimming the head and plucking bones, we are left with tender orange flesh of a fresh domesticated salmon. Wild salmon flesh is more red.

Cleaning fish requires dedication of labor time prior to service, but it is a labor not avoided or detested by cooks because of the skill and enthusiasm they enjoy. Cooks enjoy tasks requiring skill and enthusiasm away from monotonous and stodgy labors constituting most of their time. Labor tasks with enthusiasm are always a treat around the kitchen.

Prior to removing salmon from the grill, baste it with balsamic/mustard reduction sauce using a paint brush and serve immediately.

Serve with rice pilaf (prepared before service), vegetable of the night (sugar snap peas), garnish with a lemon wedge and salad greens.

For tonight's service:
18 times repeated
1 sent back to kitchen (server error in ordering)
7 complements
22% food cost

Blueberry Duck

1 package previously frozen fully cooked duck quarter
Butter
Sherry
Brandy
Caramelized Onions
Fresh Maine Blueberries
Salt
Pepper

Preparing this dish causes a philosophical dilemma for line cooks. Previously frozen fully cooked food products usually meet the passionate cook's palate with rejection, based on principle of lacking freshness. However, any line cook who respects food has a great affinity for our fine feathered friend, the duck. Tastier than chicken, more succulent than turkey, duck flesh and fat drippings make palates dance a celebration song of cheerful glee.

Many cooks are willing to overlook the previously frozen fully cooked aspect of the duck product's lacking freshness, if only for a taste of the fat drippings. Fresh duck fat is far superior to previously frozen fully cooked duck fat, but any duck fat drippings are tastier and richer than most other tolerable animal fats.

To prepare, open the previously frozen fully cooked duck package and place in a sauté pan. Place in convection oven for about 15 minutes. Remove duck and place on cutting board. Place the sauté pan with reserved duck drippings on the stove top, and heat. Pull pan away from heat and deglaze with sherry and brandy, making sure to keep one's eyebrows out of harm's way.

Put sauté pan back over stove, allowing liquor flames to die down and the alcohol to reduce. Add caramelize onions (prepared before service) and fresh Maine blueberries. Squish blueberries open, exposing their blue pasty flesh into the sauce. Turn off flame and add butter until completely melted.

Cut the duck along the bone and through the joint, allowing the thigh and leg to separate into whole pieces. Place both halves of the duck atop mashed potatoes in a pyramid formation, and pour blueberry sauce over top.

Serve with vegetable of the night (sugar snap peas), and garnish with a nasturtium. It is impossible to overcook the previously frozen fully cooked duck, and a bonehead maneuver to undercook and serve it still slightly frozen. The duck never gets sent back, so it is a fairly safe dish to take credit for. Many complements from the dining room are aroused by the duck, making the preparation of it a position of high prestige.

For tonight's service:
17 times repeated for service
0 sent back to kitchen
15 complements
22% food cost

Lamb Rack
(Tonight's Special)

8 oz. lamb rack
Rosemary
Coriander
Mushrooms
Salt
Pepper
Demi-Glace
Red Wine

Lamb is a favorite dish to prepare for many line cooks, because it is more challenging and better tasting than beef. There is a delectable flavor in lamb giving it higher respect and admiration in the kitchen than other hard meats. Preparing nightly specials is fun for cooks because it varies the routine of menu items, providing a break in the monotony of culinary work. Fresh, different, and more challenging ingredients are put to into play when making something special.

To begin, the lamb rack (cleaned and trimmed prior to service) is rubbed with salt, pepper, rosemary and coriander, before placing in a searing hot sauté pan to brown the meat.

Once the lamb turns a brilliant brown color, it is flipped and placed in the oven until the meat reaches its specified temperature. It is undercooked and allowed to rest for residual cooking for several minutes.

Lamb is usually cooked to a higher temperature than beef, because lamb flesh and fat is much tougher and chewy when medium-rare. The most common temperature for lamb is medium-well.

As lamb rests on the cutting board for residual cooking, the sauté pan is placed back on the stove-top, and the reserved lamb drippings are heated. Mushrooms are placed in the lamb drippings and sautéed for about 30 seconds, before the entire pan is deglazed with red wine. The red wine is allowed to reduce into the mushrooms before two ladles of demi-glace are added.

The pan is swirled several times, adjusting salt and pepper to taste, before being poured over the lamb. Sauté cooks must be careful because lamb is frequently sent back for serving at mis-specified temperatures. The temperature of lamb is much harder to predict than beef, and much guessing is used to determine its status.

The price of this dish keeps it a less popular item than it deserves, because many customers do not wish to spend the extra money it takes to order lamb. Servers who sell the most lamb specials always get saluted by the kitchen staff, because they are doing their jobs effectively.

Serve with roasted red potatoes (prepared before service and heated upon order), steamed chard, and garnish with a parsley sprig and rosemary sticks.

For tonight's service:
12 times repeated
1 sent back to kitchen
11 complements
30% food cost

Sugar Snap Peas
(Vegetable of the Night)

Sugar Snap Peas (picked, washed, and lightly blanched before service)
Aji-Mirin
Brown Bean Paste
Mustard
Vegetable Oil
Salt
Pepper
Soy Sauce

    Sugar snap peas are crisp and tasty, and one of the easier vegetables to prepare for line cooks on a busy Friday night. They go over well with the customers, as they have a very popular taste and remain familiar to common palates.

    They are served with nearly every entree dish, except for the specials. They are easy to prepare, but the shear number of times they need to be made makes them a labor strain at different times throughout the night. Remembering to fire peas when needed is perhaps the most difficult challenge with the vegetable "du jour".

    First, vegetable oil is heated in a sauté pan. The blanched peas are added and cooked for about 45 seconds. The pan is deglazed with aji-mirin and two splashes of water, allowing to reduce for 30 seconds, before a brown bean and mustard paste (prepared before service) is added and incorporated into the pan. Flavor is adjusted with salt, pepper, and soy sauce. The peas can be held for about 10 minutes to serve, but after this time frame they become soggy and must be thrown out, and a new order must be fired.

For tonight's service:
188 times repeated
1 sent back to kitchen (requested steamed chard)
A plethora of complements
12% food cost

Crab Cake Appetizer

2 crab cakes (prepared before service)
Olive Oil
Butter
Roasted Red Pepper Aioli (prepared before service)

A very easy and fast appetizer to make, the real labor of the crab cakes comes during the preparation hours before service. Crab cakes must be mixed together (eggs, bread crumbs, mayonnaise, seasoned salt, green pepper, red pepper, salt, pepper, onion, and fresh crab meat) before being measured into their specified portions.

Cooks don't necessarily mind cooking crab cakes, but the sheer number of them can make it a nauseating experience. The most popular appetizer on the menu, its inventory can be depleted expeditiously on busy nights. Crab cakes have a habit of burning when not given the utmost of attention, in which case they are served burn side down in hopes the customer will not notice.

Customers enjoy them immensely, and crab cakes are an excellent money maker for the restaurant. The food cost is low compared to its proportional price, and the cakes remain fresh due to the volume in which they are consumed.

Fresh batches are made nearly everyday because of their popularity. However, popularity has many drawbacks. Crab cakes are ordered so frequently throughout the night that many cooks will shout obscenities at them. Crab cakes are the most scorned victims of verbal assault on the menu, if only because they are the most popular, with service both in the lounge and dining room. If crab cakes had feelings, they would be very injured by the adjectives cooks have used to describe them. Without remorse or restraint, cooks administer verbal abuse on the crab cakes to vent their stress and frustration of working in a hot kitchen. An easy target and always remaining within frequent eye contact of cooks, crab cakes have assumed the position of scapegoat for stress and mishap.

The repetition of heating a pan of oil/butter, placing two crab cakes in the pan, sauté until brown, flip, place in the oven, and serve over a bed of greens and a side of roasted red pepper aioli with a lemon garnish, becomes a boring and tiresome ordeal. Customers really enjoy crab cakes, assuring their continued presence on the menu for future time to come. Which is a good thing, if only to assure a cook's mental health and stress exertion.

Other appetizers include: steamed mussels, skewered filet mignon pieces, skewered chicken pieces, shrimp cocktail, pan seared scallops, calamari, and a grilled vegetable medley with creamy dipping sauce. Each appetizer item is fast and easy to prepare, but repetition can prove itself a great obstacle in preserving one's sanity.

For tonight's service:
72 times repeated for service (all appetizer items combined)
0 sent back to kitchen
4 complements
Food cost varies between 4%-15%

Fried Haddock Sandwich
(Lounge Food)

4 oz. portion of Haddock (battered and breaded prior to service)
Bun
Lettuce
Tomato
Onion
Tartar Sauce
French Fries
Lemon Wedge

One of the more popular items on the lounge menu is the fried haddock sandwich. People in New England love their haddock, and people everywhere love their fish cooked in the murky depths of a deep fryer. Easy and fast, cooks enjoy orders for fried fish sandwiches because of the speed and ease of which it is prepared.

Cooks also eat a large number of fried haddock sandwiches themselves, snacking throughout the night on crispy fish flesh.

The most tedious aspect of preparing fish sandwiches is getting the plate arranged and ready for serving. Arranging lettuce, tomato and onion; grilling the bun, and reaching for a lemon wedge sounds easy enough, but can be quite an ordeal after copious repetition with many other simultaneous tasks at hand. French fries are timed with the fish, ensuring they are hot and crispy when served.

The frequency of this sandwich depends on the particular night; some nights will entail up to 20 sandwich orders, other nights will account for less than three. Either way it is a money wash for the restaurant, as the scraps from the haddock entree are crossed-utilized for the sandwich.

Hamburgers and chicken sandwiches are prepared on the grill using the same lettuce, tomato, and onion arrangement, except they usually get cheese and bacon on top and are served without tartar sauce or a lemon wedge. Other lounge items include: fresh fruit plate, cheese plate, raw vegetable plate, mozzarella sticks, barbequed pork loin, onion rings, fried (previously frozen) processed chicken strips, buffalo chicken wings, nachos, and other assorted (previously frozen) heavily salted processed items plumaged into the deep fryer.

Served with a variety of sauces including but not excluding: bleu cheese dressing, ranch dressing, hot red pepper sauce, barbeque sauce, ketchup, mustard, mayonnaise, and honey mustard (mustard and mayonnaise with honey).

For tonight's service:
54 times repeated for all sandwiches combined
39 times repeated for all other appetizers
2 sent back to kitchen (all overcooked hamburgers)
3 complements
Food cost varies between 8%-18%

House Salad

Green Leaf lettuce
Romaine lettuce
Mixed field greens
Tomatoes
Carrot shavings
Cucumber
Salt
Pepper
Dressing of choice

Being a pantry cook is a position causing great controversy in the kitchen. Pantry cooks work just as hard as line cooks, and have an overwhelming amount of prep work to perform before service begins.

And yet they must fight back against the jocular respect they receive from co-workers. Because they aren't forced to perform their work under the sauna of radiating convection heat, and not subject to the burns and sweat of a sauté cook, they can be a target of admiration. They are subject to the same amount of stress and immediacy to their job as any sauté or grill cook, but lack the grit accompanying much of a cook's charm.

Mixing salad seems easy enough to do, but mixing numerous salads for both the lounge and dining room while simultaneously preparing cold appetizers can be challenging. The greatest challenge to a pantry cook is the labor hours expended before service begins, preparing and stowing food items. The pantry cook has to prepare and stow all the salad dressings; wash, dry, and cut all the vegetables; prepare and stow various items such as croutons, hard boiled eggs, and candied almond slivers; as well as the preparation of cold appetizers and garnishes.

The pantry cook has to roast garlic and cut cheese for the cheese plate, blanch shrimp for the shrimp cocktail, and precook the chicken for grilled chicken salads. Respect is earned for the hard work of a pantry cook, but it is not without jocular admiration from those who do it in front of an oven. Salad cooks also work alongside dessert cooks, and the two normally form a bond unseen anywhere else in the kitchen.

House Salad: place lettuce mixture into a bowl with prepared vegetables. Place a dollop of dressing (ranch, bleu cheese, balsamic vinaigrette, honey-tarragon vinaigrette, or thousand island) with salt and pepper, and mix together. Place onto a chilled plate, filtering it into the center to achieve as much height to the salad as possible.

Other salads include: caesar (romaine hearts, prepared caesar dressing, parmesan cheese, croutons), spinach salad (honey tarragon vinaigrette, bacon bits, roasted red peppers, and goat cheese).

Desserts include: cheese cake, carrot cake, tiramisu, crème brûlée, chocolate mousse cake, and lemon raspberry cake. All need to be cut in precision with an artistic display of garnishing sauces on the chilled plate. Every dessert is garnished with fresh fruit, and some with flakes of white chocolate.

For tonight's service:
147 times repeated (salads, cold appetizers, desserts included)
2 sent back to kitchen (too much pepper on one salad, the wrong dressing on another)
1 complement
Food cost varies between 3%-18%

A Whiff of
Fresh Air

"I'll need to see a computer ticket for the food you ordered if you want me to prepare it. I'm not allowed to distribute food without proper documentation. Sorry, but rules are rules, no matter how practical deviation may seem at certain moments", Scott announced after Steven attempted the faux pas of verbally ordering a food item without documenting it through the computer system of inventory.

Steven had originally made an error when ordering an entree for a customer, and to speed the process, was hoping Scott could correct the error without first going through the computer. Steven's hopes had proven wrong, as Scott would not allow him a haddock when his previous order clearly stated filet mignon. More importantly, the Homestead management would come to know of this error, and hold Steven responsible for the loss of profit and food cost. Food orders ought to be impeccably accurate, as defined by the server's job description. Steven would have to suffer humiliation from his co-workers as a result of his error, but it could be worse. He could be flogged with a weighted whip.

Steven shouted in response, "I'm just so busy right now! Can't we put the rules aside just once? Can't you see what kind of dire situation I'm in right now? Alright, I'll go put it through the computer, but can you at least start so the haddock is not any more tardy than it already is? What if I were starving and poor, and I came to your backdoor. Would you feed this omnivore?" Steven asked as he began the process of documenting his food order. He's a poet in his spare time.

"It would depend. Do you have the proper documentation for receiving food from the inventory system? Have you paid your debt to society, the fee for receiving food? And if not, have you received the proper permission from an authority figure with the power to bypass the system? Have you put me in any kind of jeopardy of losing my job?", Scott replied as he seasoned the sugar snap peas. A dedicated member of the Homestead team, Scott upholds the rules and attitudes inherent to his job position.

"You would ask me those questions if I were poor and starving? You would hesitate to aid a friend in dire need?", Steven said with raised eyebrows and an askant tone of voice.

"Friends who don't comply to the rules and do not support their own competency are not friends. Friends who urge you to deviate from the system are enemies. Basically, I don't have a choice because my dedication to the Homestead is much stronger than my dedication to you. Safety is found in society, not individualism", Scott replied in laconic tones.

Not having a choice or the time to argue the issue, Steven stomped off to the dining room miffed at Scott's rigid compliance to rules. At least Steven had his haddock properly documented. No need discussing dire predicaments he will never be in, an ideology he can never change, and an expediter capable of kamikaze missions for the leader. Life is just too demanding, and table 8 needs another round of drinks.

Chef Gregg began to reminisce to Wendy about his time in the military. "One summer, right after I got out of the military, I worked on a paving crew constructing highways in Virginia. I was young, full of energy, and in need of work after returning from Okinawa, Japan. I also needed to get an ex-girlfriend out of my head. I needed to get away from girls, parties, and guns. My father knew the foreman of a paving crew, and I went to see him early one morning. I remember meeting him and asking if I could start working. 'I just want to work', I said. 'I'll learn anything I need to and work as hard as I can", Gregg began his story with optimism of its outcome. Gregg has come to thoroughly enjoy sharing life stories with Wendy, as a way to bond the two kitchen executives while preparing food.

"You were in the military?", Doug questioned without hesitation between spinach and caesar salads.

"Yup, just like my father. Except my father decided to make a career out of it. I spent four years in the marine corps, went to Japan and stayed there for about a year and a half. Had the best time of my life. Joining the marines was the best decision this 18 year old kid could have made for himself", Gregg spoke as he juiced several lemons. Doug nodded his head as he learned more about his chef's history.

"I never knew you were an ex-marine. You don't really look like one. I always figured you to be more of a jock, or maybe a disgruntled yuppy", Kendra added as she placed a filet mignon on a garnished plate, ready for expediting.

"There's no such thing as an ex-marine. You either are or you aren't. Once a marine, always a marine", Gregg said with a smile. His membership in the marine corps is a pride to last him beyond death. The thought of being a marine, bonding with his marine comrades, and possessing a marine's stories to tell always put a smile on his face.

Scott exploded, "A message to all the wait staff: I cannot give out free food, food not documented, or food intended for anything else than its sale to paying customers. If there is any left over food at the end of the night, we have permission to give you some if the situation is warranted, but do not expect anything. Make sure your personal food supply is well stocked before and after work, because reliance on the Homestead may cause you death by emaciation." Scott announced to the entire wait staff, even though most could not hear him. Excess food is either eaten by the kitchen staff or thrown in the trash. The wait staff, even though they deliver food, cannot be granted direct access to it.

"What did you say, Scott? I couldn't hear you. Something about the food? Do you have samples for us to taste?", Leanna asked as she entered the kitchen looking for an extra fork. She found the fork but forgot the mustard.

"I don't have time to repeat myself. My duties are very strenuous and time is limited. If you did not hear the official announcement, ask one of your co-workers to fill in any void information. Once I have stated the rules, it becomes your responsibility to know and follow them accordingly. I no longer have liability for any errors you may commit from this moment forth, although I do have the power of enforcement shall these rules be broken", Scott announced to Leanna after she left the kitchen with her fork and without the mustard. Leanna did not hear a word of what Scott announced.

"So the foreman looked back at me and said 'you mind working 15 hour days?' And I said 'not at all, where do I start' and he said 'tomorrow morning at 6 o'clock. Don't be late', and I said 'I'm a Marine, I'll have half my day's work finished by then", Gregg now had a smile stretch across his face as Wendy continued to emulsify her sauce. The honor he received from military experience has been the most rewarding aspect of his life.

"I mean, I would love to be able to give everyone and anyone free food and equal access to food resources, but that is not a conceivable reality. The system would not persevere with so many deviations", Scott added as he fired more entree orders to Ebbi behind him. Two haddocks and a scampi.

Kendra questioned Scott's authority, "what if someone can't pay for it, doesn't work here, and doesn't know one of the authority figures well enough to receive the proper permission? Would you let them starve?", as Kendra flipped a filet mignon. Taking compassionate stances on political issues has become a common occurrence for Kendra.

"I would tell them to get a job and earn the money they need, get a job here, or become friends with authority figures. Otherwise, our state government provides soup kitchens to feed the hungry. We are not a soup kitchen, we are an independent place of business whose product is food", Scott did not hesitate with his answer, very sure of himself and the political stance he took in relation to the argument.

"So I started that next day, paving roads for the state of Virginia. Without any friends around, no women to distract me, and no where else to go, I worked 15 hours a day without any place to spend money. I worked under the grueling humid sun of a Virginia summer, surrounded by drunken construction workers and suburban landscape. Although I missed the corps, it was nice to take a break from the four year routine. The overtime hours added up fast, and before long, I had a stockpile of money no young kid ought to have. Young kids and piles of money do not last long, and never go to the right places. I was not prepared for what the future held in store for me, but at the moment, I was working everyday and piling up money I didn't know how to spend", Gregg continued.

Kendra would not let it go. "But what if the person didn't have the resources available to get money, the Homestead wasn't hiring, and the authority figures were not interested in becoming friends with this person?", Kendra seeks not to win the argument by stating a better case than Scott, but to show him the fallacies of his own argument.

"I paved roads for two months, saving money and doing nothing else. After I acquired a sizable lump of money, and I became tired of paving roads, I moved back to Maine and began my culinary career washing dishes. First in Saco, then in York, and now in Ogunquit. A long and winding road it was, no pun intended, but here I am, the chef of the Homestead and happy to be home", Gregg was reminiscing on his past and making Wendy feel more at ease about her story of invisible cream.

"Hey, if people don't want to comply with the system, they don't have to. They can leave if they don't like it. But why would I care when they suffer? Maybe once they start suffering they will realize our system wasn't so bad after all, and much of their criticism was unwarranted. If people want to contribute to society there are plenty of jobs out there. Starving stomachs are not the fault of our system, but the fault of individuals. There is no reason for emaciation in our world given the opportunities available to all", Scott was now paying more attention to Kendra than he was the flow of food orders coming back to him. He accidentally dropped a ladle, and butter splattered onto his clog.

Kendra still refused to let it go. "And let's not forget how much food our system destroys to protect and maintain market prices. How can you not see food as an essential commodity of human society? Just take a moment to reflect on how some might not be able to afford opportunities for eating", Kendra was now appealing to Scott's pathos, and he was not ready to rebut this type of appeal. It caught him off-guard. He has work to do, and now is not the time.

"What I remember most wasn't the long hours, scarce food, or the sun burn on my neck. After I left Virginia and came back to Maine, I went back to Virginia a second time the following summer to see if I could get my old job back. I wanted to buy a small house and a plot of land, and thought I could work my 15 hour days for a couple of months and make another pile of money. I saw my old boss again, and he immediately rehired me. He always thought I was a good worker, and had respect for military men, especially marines. After seeing him in the afternoon, I went to sleep that night and got up bright and early for the morning shift", the time Gregg gets to chat and reminisce about old times with co-workers is a treasure unavailable in most other workplaces.

"It's not my fault if some people in the world aren't motivated enough to feed their own mouths. Food is a business", Scott spoke with a twist of anger in his voice, but was still able to maintain the work tasks in front of him and in need of attention.

"On my first day back of the second summer, the smell of tar, which had escaped me before, was now too overpowering for me to breathe. The tar odor which had not affected me the first summer, was now inspiring nausea in my dizzy head and urges of vomit in my queasy stomach. My lungs hurt, my legs wobbled. The tar odor had not affected me the year prior because my nose became accustomed to it, dulling any sense of this odorous toxin's detection. My nose required a ten month trip to Maine for this sense to return. It's a good thing this sense was able to return, because the ability to detect poisons is a human talent of the most divine order", Gregg spoke as he deeply inhaled the scent of basil leaves cupped in his hands. "That's why I went back to the restaurant business, to inspire my nose with the delicious scents of basil, garlic, and olive oil".

"If you were able to sense tar upon returning, why couldn't you detect it the first year? It seems as though the consciousness of toxic odor would have been overwhelming the initial day of work. Yet you worked all those hours for a whole summer, and the toxic fumes were not a problem. How could this be?", Wendy asked with a voice of sympathy and curiosity over her question.

"Distracted, I guess. I came to the Virginia Department Of Transportation for reasons much deeper than the aspiration of laying tar and constructing roads. I don't remember the odor being quite so overwhelming the first year, being distracted by my ex-girlfriend and leaving the military. I didn't care about the ingestion of poison, I only cared about distracting my thoughts. Health and longevity were not a priority", Gregg replied to Wendy.

"But not every impoverished person partakes in theft and debauchery, and every debaucherist does not want to be impoverished. We are all family, and we must support our family members if we are to attain the future potential of humanity", Kendra now spoke for the people who did not have a voice in the discussion.

"What does debauchery have to do with food? Make up your mind, and don't confuse different ends of argument. How a person acts is who a person is. Are you trying to say ignorance relates to emaciation? What exactly are you accusing me of?", Scott now took a defensive stance against the words of Kendra, attacking her point of view by doubting the consistency of her argument.

"My nose could not withstand the noxious tar odor any longer. My stomach turned and my legs became dizzy with each passing breath of inhaled tar fumes. I tried not to let it bother me, if only to show my comrades I was tough. After only 35 minutes I felt the urge to vomit. The dizziness and nausea became more than I could bear. I stumbled back to the foreman and said I couldn't work anymore. The fumes had become too overpowering. I had to stop", Gregg stared blindly into the wall, chopping the basil he inhaled just moments before.

"That's interesting. I wonder what that meant while you were working the first summer. Just because you couldn't smell the fumes doesn't mean they were any less poisonous, only that you couldn't sense them. I wonder if any damage to your lungs occurred from the first summer of exposure?", Wendy spoke with a tone of relief for the fortunate ending to Gregg's story.

"Don't talk to me about turtles and rabbits, because I think it's a bunch of nonsense, anyway. People are who they are and will behave how they are going to behave, and if they don't like being labeled, then they ought to change. Otherwise they will be forced to deal with what their behavior has awarded them", Scott said as he dodged a flame created by the brandy Ebbi splashed into his sauté pan. Not paying attention, he accidentally bumped his head into the hood vent.

Wendy replied to Gregg deep in thought. "There's something about false security in your story. Something about perceptions and practical reality. How we perceive not what truth is telling us, but how our distractions can guide us into false security. Your nose had the ability to sense tar fumes the first year of paving roads in Virginia, but distraction trumped its talent", Wendy spoke with a glazed look in her eye, trying to figure out the story Gregg spoke of. She knew Gregg had related both their stories together, and wanted to know how tar fumes relate to a little naked girl dancing around the house with invisible cream.

"I just hope you don't judge your friends and family in this way. I hope you aren't injuring yourself by injuring others with your power of thought and access to the food supply", Kendra spoke as she flipped a salmon filet.

Scott was not about to let it go. "I'm sorry, but this is my job and I am required to perform it. And if you don't like the ideology accompanying it, then go somewhere else. This is who I am, and I am not going to change. If jobs and job occupations create ideologies you don't agree with, then I can do nothing for you. This is the way things are. Learn to live with it", Scott replied in an effort to end the argument.

"What is your job description, anyway?", Ebbi asked of Scott. Scott turned around and looked at Ebbi, pausing from his shouting of food orders. Scott glanced at Ebbi, then back at the sugar snap peas, then back at Ebbi again.

"I'm an expediter", Scott said.

"But what is the job description of expediter? What does it mean to have the identity of expediter?" Ebbi asked while flipping shrimp in a sauté pan.

"He doesn't know", Kendra spoke between burger flips. "Hey chef, do you have the job description of expediter? Can you bring out the file describing Scott's occupation? We would love to see it".

"Yes, I have everyone's job description. And yes, I can sense what my nose smells. As soon as I finish chopping the basil I will retrieve it", Gregg smiled at Wendy as he spoke these words. Most of the kitchen did not know what he was talking about. Wendy took the chopped basil to the refrigerator and covered it with a wet paper towel, while Gregg walked towards his office to fetch the expediter's job description.

Expediter

Expediter, oh my expediter. The backbone of efficient kitchen, voice of all to hear. Reader of tickets, distributor of food. Keeper of order. Dictating system flow. Enforcer of rules. Speaks through monetary language, speaks through technology device. Administrator of political climate, supporter of status quo. Protector.

Expediter, oh my expediter. Powers possessed. Feed our stomachs. What would we do without you? Our foundation of order. Shouts instructions to cooks. Responsible for food's movement and presentation.

The Homestead is a warehouse of food. The expediter its gatekeeper. A warehouse whose access is through a small door. A small door guarded by the expediter. Food must be distributed with piety to law of political economy. Some will suffer. Others prosper. The system is safe.

Food
Philosophy

Vegetables and Herbs

Vegetables and herbs are the mainstay of human diet, and ought to be consumed in generous quantities. Nature exists in its purest form inside vegetables, and their bounty was created to be consumed as such. The labor needed to grow vegetables encourages the natural tendencies of humans to gather together in groups, as gardening is a natural communal effort.

No food brings humans together quite like vegetables. To cultivate nutrition as well as community, it remains imperative that vegetable consumption does not come from processing factories, rotten resources, or sprouted from perverted seeds. When utilized successfully, a garden and its vegetables have the potential to be a metaphor for family, town, or a nation.

Vegetables are very digestible in the human digestive tract, as they contain high quantities of water and fibrous earth. Nutritional benefits vary amongst individual vegetables, but they all remain in high spiritual order of not only physical nutrients, but metaphoric nourishment as well.

Vegetables yield many benefits to human bodies including: greater ease of urination and defecation, optimal oral hygiene, serene stomachs, increased blood circulation, and the bathing of precious organs in metaphor.

Vegetables harvest high amounts of energy in humans because of their high water content. A person consuming large amounts of fresh vegetables free of pesticides, chemical washes, and artificial dyes will have many years of healthy life.

Fruits

Fruits are high in water content, possessing large amounts of water held together by loose earthy fibers. Water has a high rate of mobility inside the fruit (as it grows), and this high rate of water movement translates itself once ingested in the human body.

Once ingested, the fruit's water circulates very quickly in the body. Fruits are an admirable source of quick energy. The different colors of fruit symbolize the variance in water content, as the color of each fruit varies according to how the water is held and how the water flow is conducted internally.

Eating a moderate and consistent amount of fruits is ideal for the human digestive system, but eating too many will cause a sudden burst of energy, excessive urinating, and cramping of the kidney. The high sugar content of fruits is nutritious, but can become a detriment if not moderated. Fruits are to be eaten less frequently than vegetables, but more frequently the roots, spices, and nuts. As with vegetables, eating fruits not saturated in pesticides, preservatives, dyes, chemical washes, or sprouted from perverted seeds is necessary to reduce the incidence of illness and ailment. The natural tastiness of fruits will be enough to make a palate dance without manipulating its natural flavor.

Roots, Spices, and Nuts

Roots, spices, and nuts are very fibrous and high in earthy structure. Incorporating them into the diet will yield high nutritional value, holding water together inside the body and aiding excretion processes. Because they possess high amounts of fiber and low water, their main benefit is to help the logistics of digestion.

Eating too many earthy foods can cause discomfort of the gastrointestinal tract, as a disproportionate amount of earth compared to water will eschew the balance of intestinal harmony. Eating the wrong earthy foods can cause allergic reactions when fibers do not combine with the water of a body in a beneficial way.

To best ingest earthy foods such as roots, nuts, and spices, incorporation into sauces, soups, and seasonings is largely preferred by most cultures, as eating highly fibrous foods is generally too overwhelming for comfortable ingestion. Flavoring foods with high fibers will also greatly enhance the palate appeal of recipes, making tasty what would otherwise be boring or inedible.

Fish

Fish is different than other fleshy meats of the earth, especially for humans, because they possess a high amount of water as compared to hard meats and poultry. Fish are animals who live in water, and it is only natural for them to possess a higher amount of water content than other land dwelling or flighted creatures.

A soft and highly digestible flesh, fish provides humans with an ease of digestion and copious amounts of nutritional value conducive to the human digestive system. Eating fish provides humans with digestible protein, soluble earth, as well as the metaphoric essence of an ocean, lake, or river.

Lean and tasty, fish have won over the world with its appeal. Fish is a meat unrestricted by any culture or religion of the world (as is many other assorted meats), and is known to be the bearer of nutritional satiation if a culture is lucky enough to be in proximity to substantial fish sources.

Fish are water creatures, and given that humans are composed of nearly three quarters water content and require the ingestion of water for physical health, it is only natural in assuming fish to be a beneficial food source.

Grains and Starches

Grains and starches provide humans with hearty earthy fibers. Grains and starches provide a practical filling of the belly, and even though largely lacking nutritional value as compared to fruits, fish, and vegetables, they provide an energy source and satiation of emotional needs.

Starches serve as sponges in the body, a characteristic with the potential to be a great asset or detriment to a human's health. Eaten in moderation, starches will absorb the nutritious water of other foods and carry them through the digestive tract, distributing nutrition and energy evenly throughout the digestive process. Eaten in excess, grains and starches will dehydrate the body and overload the intestines, causing discomforts in the gastrointestinal tract, difficult bowel movements, sleepiness, and dehydration.

It is not uncommon for people to develop allergies or intolerance to certain grains and starches. Cramping, gas, heartburn, dehydration, energy loss, and weight gain are results of choosing grains unwisely or excessively. Every culture around the world has a particular variety of grain they eat as a staple in their diet, as grains feed the bulk of the world's hunger and satiate images of home and bounty.

Faans

It is unfortunate the word "fat" is a homonym in the English language. "Fat" the nutrient is much different than "fat" the condition of obesity. Because of this unfortunate error of the language, many people have avoided this nutrient for mistakenly believing it to cause obesity.

We shall now use the acronym "F.A.A.N." (Fat As A Nutrient) to avoid any more unfortunate misunderstandings. Faans are important components of a healthy human diet, and must be ingested to provide many different health benefits.

Faans provide lubrication for foods traveling through the intestines, coating the stomach lining and intestines with a shield of protection. Just as oils are an essential component for the health of hydrating skin to lock in water moisture, oils are necessary for the stomach and intestines to lock in their own essential water moisture.

Faans provide lubrication and maintain the presence of water. Water and oil repel each other, but work in a symbiotic relationship when in balance. The skin is an excellent example. Because oil and water don't mix, skin oil acts as a protective shield locking in hydration where it is needed.

In deciding what faans to eat and which fats to avoid, a good indication is their form at room temperature. Most faans that are liquid at room temperature are usually considered healthy. In general, the higher quality of faan, the more benefit it will provide. Liquid oils are good examples of faans at room temperature. Solid faans such as lard, butter, and shortening ought to be avoided because they can stick to the intestinal lining excessively.

The faans taken from fresh fruits, nuts, and vegetables provide excellent nutrition and symbiotic relationships to water inside the body, and ought to be consumed in adequate but moderate amounts. Fish fat is the softest animal faan for a human to consume, and yields optimal nutrition even though it is not a liquid.

Poultry, Hard Meat

The ingestion of winged and feathered creatures is more digestible than hard meats like beef, but not as digestible as fish. The tastiness of poultry is a pleasant contradiction to the watery flesh of fish. In most every way, poultry is a middle point between fish and hard meat in relation to water and earth composition, as well as the dynamics of ingestion in the human body.

Water

Water is the most important nutrient for a human body to digest, but the methods of ingestion can be commonly misunderstood. Ingesting water correctly is just as important as the nutritional value of water itself. Many people falsely believe drinking large amounts of liquid water will make them hydrated and healthy. This is not necessarily true.

Being hydrated is more involved than simply drinking water. Actually, drinking large amounts of water will have the reverse affect on the body, and will lead to its unhealthy opposite of dehydration.

If a person drinks too much liquid water, many nutrients of the body, including faans, will be washed away into the excessive urination to follow. Much of the body's earth holding the water in place will be washed away, leaving the body unable to hold water together at all. Much like the skin wrinkling and drying when exposed to excess water, the internal body works the same. Water is useless to a human body if it does not have the earth to hold it together and the oil to lock it in place.

To ingest water without washing away earth and oil, and to attain the state of hydration, four steps must be followed:

1) Ingest foods with high water content
2) Ingest moderate amounts of liquid water
3) Ingest foods with earthy fibers and faans
4) Do not be dehydrated

The fourth item above is more complicated than expected. Being hydrated is very much about not being dehydrated. Not ingesting dehydrating foods and drinks, not partaking in dehydrating activities, not washing away the earth of the body. The body will naturally maintain its salubrious water volumes, and we must allow our bodies to be as natural as they can by not being dehydrated.

Dialectic Conversations: Earth and Water

After a long day of work, Ebbi sits down at his computer and begins to chat with a friend over the internet.

Ebbi: Human flesh and organ are made of an abundant three quarters water content, a proportion not to be denied or trivialized into irrelevancy. But let us not limit our thoughts of water to include human flesh and organ exclusively, for all animals, creatures, and plants share the same divine homage to water. Plants even more so than humans, for plant flesh is known to possess in abundance of nine tenths water content, an amount too astounding to be ignored.

Antiphia: So you are stating, as life on this earth, we owe our existence to the presence of water? That water is the divine presence in all earthly life, and our understanding of it will shed light on our consciousness? Are you to say, given your emphasis on the water composition of all living things, that we are all merely different forms of water?

Ebbi: Yes, but not exclusively. It is not enough to simply state all living creatures are different forms of water without first understanding the nature of water and its balancing opposite. Water, in the sense of divinity, is not limited exclusively to the common forms of water; such as liquid water, ice, steam, lakes, clouds, and rain; it is these forms but also a divine spirit and replenishment of eternal energy. The spirit of water is constantly moving, constantly replenishing, constantly flowing. Examples of this spirit can be understood in the external world of oceans, rivers, creeks, ponds, puddles, snow, ice, vapor, rain, condensation, clouds, aquifers, groundwater, drips, drops, and splatters. The spirit of water in the external world is an everlasting and omnipresent power superceding all life as we know it. But just as water exists in our external world, it also resides in the internal world of our bodies. Water flows, replenishes, and invigorates the internal body just as it does the ocean and rain.

Antiphia: So tell me then, why does water not come to life when I hold it in my mouth, lather it on my skin, or see its majesty crashing on the ocean shores?

Ebbi: To explain this, I will need to demonstrate the duality of water energy. Water could not exist by itself, and relies on the opposite energy of earth to maintain its inspired form. The duality consisting of both water and earth creates life, a duality working simultaneously to produce what we know as existence.

Antiphia: Please, continue your explanation. Continue the explanation of water and earth in its inspired forms.

Ebbi: First we must expand our definition of what water and earth are commonly known to be. Water is not only common rain, lakes, and ice; earth is not merely common soil, minerals, and rock.

Antiphia: I am waiting to hear what this expanded definition ought to be. I have only known these elements as the common forms you have described, and do not understand them as anything more divine.

Ebbi: We must understand not only the physical forms of these elements, but the spirit natural to each. It is important to remember, harmony possesses a spirit in excess of its two parts. The harmony of water and earth in its particular forms is the inspiration of life.

Antiphia: I have understood the words you speak, but my thinking is at a loss for practical examples of how this union of harmony relates to the nature of existence. How and why do water and earth unite to form the inspiration of life?

Ebbi: We shall use an example of the human body to illustrate our point.

Antiphia: Please, proceed.

Ebbi: Is not the human body recognized to be composed in excess of three quarters water content?

Antiphia: Yes, this is a basic form of knowledge.

Ebbi: That indeed, and without doubt, the vast composition of our flesh and organs is due to this abundant water content?

Antiphia: Yes. No person could argue these common facts against you with any success.

Ebbi: Excellent. Let us take one body part in particular to examine before expanding our discussion to include the complete body.

Antiphia: Is it alright if I select the particular body part to discuss? I would like to exemplify the eyeball and how it relates to water and earth.

Ebbi: The eyeball will work very well to illustrate our example.

Antiphia: I am listening with great anticipation, and I give you an eyeball.

Ebbi: Let us begin. Could we not view the eyeball as a wonderful and mysterious organ of the body, an organ with talents to sense color, movement, shades, and emotional expressions in others? Could we not say eyeball talents are beyond duplication of human technology, and we owe gratitude to conception for giving us the great sense of vision? Its abilities to decipher light from dark, red from blue, and sadness from happiness in others, are of a divine form? And the physical position of the eyeball in the skull, the eyelids protecting it, and the retina covering the pupil, are also divine attributes of the eyeball? Is not the eyeball, by all stretches of rational thought, a heavenly creation residing within our bodies?

Antiphia: I cannot argue any assertions so far. What you say of the eyeball is true beyond all doubt, and beyond any worthy rebuttal.

Ebbi: And even though we say these divine talents exist within the eye, if we were to take the eyeball and dissect it, we would find no revelation of its mysterious secrets? That indeed, the eyeball is recognized as being composed of nearly nine tenths water content, and one tenth earthy fibers. If we were to open an eyeball, a plethora of water, earthy fibers, and empty space would spill out and nothing more.

Antiphia: Correct. This is a great obstacle scientists and doctors have encountered when studying and understanding the human body and how its talents work. The talents of the eyeball, or any other human organ, do not seem to make sense when their entire content is water and fiber.

Ebbi: A dilemma indeed, because these scientists and doctors do not understand the delicate and eternal balance of water and earth, nor the harmony of spirit produced when united. It is upon the philosophers to understand such a harmony and make light where others cast dark.

Antiphia: And this is our intention for understanding? To shed light on internal energies and rhythms of the earth, to understand body dynamics?

Ebbi: Exactly. Water is eternally alive and active, no matter what form it exists. The dynamics of water on the external earth are the same dynamics of the internal human body. Is it not true, observing the ocean, to say it never stands still? Is not the ocean eternally alive and active? Are not waves, currents, rips, and tides omnipresent across the entire ocean with ceaseless energy?

Antiphia: Indeed, I have never seen the ocean at rest. Water seems to possess an eternal spirit inspiring it into activity. Even the vast amount of ice caught in glaciers breathes a spirit of eternal life.

Ebbi: And if we are to make the same eternal claim over other forms of water, would we stray from the truth? Is it not true that rain, mist, clouds, lakes, vapor, rivers, snow, and hail also possess an eternal spirit like the ocean?

Antiphia: We would certainly not stray from the truth in making such claims.

Ebbi: And if we are to view the external forms of water in such a way, why would our internal forms of water be any different? Could we not claim the water content of our eyeball to possess the same energy of the ocean?

Antiphia: Certainly, this follows. Humans are part of this earth and not fragmented from it.

Ebbi: As earth creatures, we are not separated from the virtues of nature, but a part of its vast eternally replenishing system.

Antiphia: Nature is most certainly within us, as the state of nature would not make sense if it were not. The truth you speak certainly exists where you say it does, for if they did not, nature would be a chaotic mess of confusion and collective fallacy.

Ebbi: So we may say the spirit of water gives the eyeballs its talent? That certainly, an energy divine enough to inspire the omnipresent ocean could very well inspire the eyeball?

Antiphia: Yes, this may be concluded, for if water is powerful enough to inspire the ocean and rain, it is certainly powerful enough to inspire the eyeball. But many questions remain before I can thoroughly accept this answer. How is eyeball water formed in one place and not another? Why is there a difference of talent between the eyeball and the liver, even though both are composed of a majority water? Why is the water in my drinking glass not an eyeball? Surely if the eyeball is nine tenths water and one tenth earthy fibers, the liver will be composed of nearly identical proportions of water and earth. What inspires the difference of physical form and talent?

Ebbi: Excellent questions, and ones that must be answered to legitimate our argument. To answer all these questions we must take a deeper observation at water's equal opposite, earth, to reveal the answers we seek.

Antiphia: Please, continue. Describe the earth you speak of.

Ebbi: Earth is defined as an element inspiring water into its physical forms. Without earth, water would have no physical form at all. Earth is not only common soil, clay, sand, minerals, stones, and rocks; it is also air, fibers, gravity, and bones. Earth is any structure providing water with a physical form, and therefore, is as omnipresent as water in the natural world.

Antiphia: Although I can readily admit to understanding earth in the forms you speak of, I do not see which direction you are taking this reasoning. To clarify, relate these concepts back to our example of the eyeball.

Ebbi: Very well. There are two basic elements composing the eyeball: water and earth. The spirits of both harmonize their energies to form the talent of the eyeball. If not for the eyeball fibers, the eyeball waters would not be inspired to pursue eyeball talents. If not for the eyeball waters, the eyeball fibers would dry and disintegrate. Clearly, each side of the duality is dependent on the other for existence.

Antiphia: I see. There are two ingredients in the construction of organs: earth and water. Inside these two ingredients are spirits relating to each. And the harmonized product of the two ingredients is a spiritual energy exceeding the power of the two ingredients individually. The different talents of each different organ is based on the particular harmony of earthy fibers and water. Of which there are countless variations depending on how, and under what conditions of inspiration, earth and water harmonized.

Ebbi: Precisely. The different fibers of earth inspire the particular inspirations of water. Eyeball fibers inspire water into eyeball talents, liver fibers inspire water into liver talents, brain fibers inspire water into brain talents. Once inspired water unifies with earthy fibers, future potential is conceived.

Antiphia: I am beginning to understand. May we also conclude this interplay of earth and water to be relevant for animals, fish, insects, plants, and all other earthly life?

Ebbi: Absolutely, without any hesitation.

Antiphia: And each particular organ of every earthly life shows this in common?

Ebbi: Yes, but let us not limit our thinking to fragmented parts of the body. We must also be aware of earth and water inspiration of complete body dynamics.

Antiphia: What do we need to be conscious of when relating dynamics to complete bodies?

Ebbi: Recall what we have discussed earlier of water and how we applied it to the talents of the eyeball. Recall also the eternal and omnipresent spirit in water. This spirit not only applies to individual fragmented pieces of the body, but works with complete body dynamics as well.

Antiphia: Please, speak further. I would like to know how complete dynamics work concerning the spirited flow of earth and water.

Ebbi: Just as water flows and inspires the individual eyeball, water flows and inspires throughout the entire body. Our discussion of the eyeball will no longer be seen as a fragmented piece of the body, but as one function within a working body.

Antiphia: Proceed. I am anxious to see the direction of our discussion.

Ebbi: Would the eyeball not cease to exist if the entire body were to perish?

Antiphia: Most definitely. The eyeball is dependent on the complete health of the body. Without the body, the eyeball would certainly perish.

Ebbi: Is it relevant to say, based on your agreements, that the eyeball is reliant on the health and well-being of the stomach, pancreas, and spine for its own health and longevity?

Antiphia: Very relevant. Certainly the organs you have listed contribute to overall health, and each are dependent on the others for life.

Ebbi: Then we can say it is important for water to flow, not only internal to the eyeball, but within the entire body as well? Can we say the flow of water does not only exist in the eyeball for the eyeball, but for the universe inside a body?

Antiphia: It sounds as though you are comparing ocean water with body water. This is an exquisite metaphor in describing the deeper significance of dynamics as related to fragmented pieces. Ocean water not only exists for the ocean, but for the dynamics of all nature on earth.

Ebbi: Exactly. Blood flow can be seen as an example of this metaphor. Blood flow works to unify the entire cosmos of the body in eternal flow. It is a communication between all parts of the body. The higher the clarity, the higher the flow of blood and essential health.

Antiphia: So blood flow is the ultimate substance of energy in the body?

Ebbi: No, blood flow is only a metaphor illustrating the flow of water within the body. Water is the ultimate substance of energy in the body, superceding blood for its rooted foundation in existence.

Antiphia: Please, then, explain how water flows in the body.

Ebbi: Water flows like blood and is grounded like earth. It is invisible to the naked vision of the eye, but clear to a healthy conscious. It is the connection, communication, and common thread between all organs and spirit of life.

Antiphia: Understanding water will allow us to better understand the nature of our bodies?

Ebbi: Precisely.

Antiphia: I am both hesitant and anxious to ask if there are any deeper notions pertaining to the flow of water in the body. Are there any deeper concepts of water we have not discussed, shedding light on deeper consciousness of truth?

Ebbi: Yes, but these deeper concepts are much more difficult to understand, and the prior concepts must be understood initially before further progress can be made.

Antiphia: I beg to know, what are these deeper concepts you speak of?

Ebbi: There is a flow of energy throughout the body invisible to the naked eye, but relevant to the consciousness. It is a field of energy paths water flows throughout and within. We cannot analyze or dissect this energy, because its existence is not in tangible form, and transforms itself upon death. It flows like water and guides like earth, but is neither and both simultaneously. Water flow creates an energy inspiring our current existence and replenishing itself for future endeavors. Purpose, meaning, and enigmas of life will come to light when conscious of duality's flow.

Antiphia: So there is a purpose of life to be deduced from the wisdom of water and earth? A gateway to the root of our existence?

Ebbi: Yes. As living creatures our birth was an expression of this duality. Uncovering the substance of our birth conception will yield answers to our many questions of confusion. We are to live our lives thinking and acting like the flow of water and earth united, so we may return to the earth as peacefully and harmoniously as we arrived.

Antiphia: The purpose of our life is to die?

Ebbi: No. It is to be aligned with water/earth duality so we may be content and healthy during our existence and eventually die a peaceful death, returning to the earth and water from which we sprouted. Food plays a key role in our lives for this reason as a metaphor for aligned duality. Food ought to flow through our bodies like the water and earth of inspiration, so our life will flow with greater ease and future potential will be satiated.

Pens & Carrots

"Look under the counter, will you Kurt? I dropped my pen and I need it back. A server without a pen is like a writer without vision. Communication is worthless without the proper tool to use. I would feel so very naked without my beloved pen in hand, and a woman ought never be naked in public or she will cease any respectability to her name. Prospects of prostitution always hover over females in civilized society. So please, fetch my pen before female honor becomes suspect, and my name opens to insinuating assumptions of how a working woman obtains her money", as Barbara looked at Kurt with her big blue eyes.

Kurt fetched her pen if only to prevent the tragedy of hovering female character assumptions. Civilized society can be a very cruel place for the honest and decent. Although Kurt thought it odd for a person to get insinuating ideas merely seeing a woman without a pen, when the most obvious assumptions would be a woman with a pen. The phallic structure of a writing utensil could be a rich source of giggly laughs for the insinuating immature.

"Thank you Kurt. You are the best. My hero. The rescuer of pens and the protector of honor. If only you were a bit taller I would consider you a boyfriend candidate. And more wealthy. But I do enjoy your compliance to my commands, which is a very worthy character trait for a man to possess. Carrot stick?", as Barbara plunged into the plate of vegetable snacks she brings to work for grazing purposes.

The dinner shift can be long, and bellies can moan when servers smell food they mustn't touch. Carrots, cucumbers, tomatoes, and celery are on Barbara's vegetable menu today, although she does not care much for celery. For some reason she puts it on the plate anyway, if only to show others she enjoys one of the more popular root vegetables even though she doesn't. Dunking the celery in extra heavy dairy dip helps this compliance to conformity. Disguising undesired flavor to soothe the palate is key for legitimizing an often cruel civilized society.

"Don't worry about it, Barb. Just here to help. I wouldn't say I'm a savior or anything, just a friend willing to help when needed. Now, could you help me with table 19? It's a table of five people, and I can't carry all of their food at once. I wish I had the strength of Hercules, but for now I will just have to settle for his hair", Kurt asked Barbara as she finished the last chomp of her carrot stick.

He headed back to the kitchen expecting Barbara to follow behind. Five plates is dangerous to carry with its increased drop potential, and Kurt assumed he was privileged to Barbara's help if only for his courageous pen fetching and honor protecting. Barbara loves her pen. But even a courageous pen fetching warrior like Kurt could not triumph over hidden giggling, as Barbara declined her assistance for Kurt.

"Ooh, sorry Kurt. No can do. Got to go get an order from my table, using this ol' pen to make a note of it. Memory ain't so good after the accident. I'm sure one of our fine feathered comrades will be willing to help, so go ask if they are more willing and able. Cucumber?", as Barbara whisked herself away to the dining room.

Good thing Barbara's customers won't proposition her for fornication in exchange for financial compensation, thanks to the pen. The accident she spoke of occurred last week, slipping on a wet floor and falling on her butt. Normally, falling on a butt would not be a traumatic event, but being a woman, the insinuations could get out of control. Only prostitutes call attention to their butts, and only prostitutes are mocked when humiliation is afoot.

Servers at the Homestead are a collection of workers either largely educated but lacking the drive to pursue a bureaucratic desk job, college students in need fast money, drug addicts, or children of wealthy parents who use the Homestead as a cover to satisfy mom and dad well enough to stop asking when they are going finish their PhD. Other types of servers like aspiring actors, down on their luck divorced single moms, and just happy to be here middle aged hippies, do not work much at the Homestead, choosing rather to live in either

New York or California, their hometown, or whatever place their ex-romance once led them to live.

Here in coastal southern Maine, there are seasonal workers who come just for the summer beaches, and people from foreign lands on visas to collect the sinew American money so popular for its buying power. When the weather cools down and the gentle summer breeze turns into an arctic gust, many seasonal workers migrate to Florida chasing the ducks and geese to warmer waters.

The seasonally migrating workers create a labor climate to be envied by some. It helps to allow travel up and down the east coast, chasing sunny weather from north to south, and back again. Florida can be a bit too hot in summer, and Maine can be a bit too frigid in winter. The balance can be perfect at times.

There is a large population of gay men who partake in this migration, sharing their companionship in the New England and South Beach charm, where a male companion would otherwise be faux pas in civilized society. The gay population assures culture and tasteful decorating are abound, good food and a high cost of living. The gay population also makes good for women to reside, as women and gay men often make the best of friends, very close and very disclosed with one another. Where gay men reside, attractive women and dance clubs are not far away. Which makes good reason for heterosexual men to populate gay beach towns, for the sojourning women announce their availability under the sunshine of good food and tasteful decorating. Gay beach towns often frustrate a woman's sexuality, being surrounded by men who make good companions but lousy lovers. Inspiring a gay man's penis with breasts and a vagina is a losing cause, even if they do smell like flower pedals and vanilla beans. It's best to leave gay men to other gay men, avoiding the heartbreak of a person being who they were meant to be.

The migration of workers also leaves restaurant laborers vulnerable and expendable to firings from their place of employment. It is very easy for restaurants to fire an employee for fickle reasons because there are many willing workers ready to commit their loyalty at the drop of a hat. Homestead serving positions are highly sought after because of its high financial compensation compared to its labor expense, especially for a job not requiring education credentials but strangely saturated in them. Unfortunately, the toll serving tables takes on sanity can be a bit debilitating, even though the labor expense is not as rigid as many other bureaucratic jobs can be.

Serving the public can be especially stressful, especially a public eternally hungry and thirsty. People turn to ravenous beasts when their food is concerned, losing all sense of etiquette when biological desires are desperate. Especially when their money is involved. People expect their money to justify their behavior, and will lose all sense of etiquette if their money is not performing the task. Providing satiation can be a tiring task, but this is what servers are asked to do on a nightly basis. Good thing they've been to college. Bending to the whims and pleas of a whining public who are reliant on a service economy to fill their bellies is not suited for the weak of wits.

Perhaps the most difficult task of the Homestead server is acting as liaison between the public and Scott, the expediter. Communication is an essential component of any efficient society, and the Homestead is no different. The relationship between expediter and public is determined by the servers, and could very well be the difference between success and failure in the restaurant business. Without effective servers communication with food resources would be an inefficient chaos leaving an emaciated public vulnerable. If money cannot buy food it has defeated its own purposes. People would die, societies would wither. A horrible death by emaciation would be afoot.

A server brings food from the kitchen, prepared and delicious. The server is financially compensated for their service, delivering style, grace, and class along with the food. They are financially deducted for drool, boogers, hair strands, or any unappetizing habits. Good clean service, fresh from a talented kitchen, rich in the smiles of a financially driven society will yield the highest rewards for this labor.

Kurt found Steve, who appeared to be bored, and spoke to him through a voice of urgency. "Hey Steve, can you give me hand? I need to take this food to table 19, and I can't carry all five plates at once. I've been trying to grow another arm on my day off but those magic beans don't seem to work very well. Who would think they would be dud after the amount of money I paid for them", Kurt asked and joked with his distressed smile.

Kurt laid the battle plan for Steven, saying, "gray haired lady with lazy eye gets haddock, ear hair man gets salmon, the younger looking man with a Charlie Brown haircut gets beef, the younger woman with lipstick on her teeth gets chicken caesar salad, and the kid gets hamburger with french fries. All set. Ready to go", Kurt twists his foot into the floor scratching an itch on the ball of his foot before he is ready to go. He picks up three plates full of hot food, heading out toward the dining room in pursuit of table 19, Steven trailing behind him with a hamburger and chicken caesar salad.

"I'm right behind you, buddy. Let's roll it out to table 19. Hot food coming through! Service with a smile, here we come!", Steven spoke to Kurt's back as he walked behind him with the two plates he agreed to carry, relieving Kurt of the much detested second trip to the kitchen.

Not only does a second trip delay the table from initiating their collective meal and prolong emaciation, but it humiliates Kurt for not performing work tasks effectively and thoroughly, as judged by Scott. Civilized society expects men to labor effectively and thoroughly, for if he is not able, people may get insinuating ideas about his personal livelihood. And then Kurt would predictably blame his lackluster performance on the apathy of his teammates, because he asked for help and received none. Lackluster efficiency, blame, whining, and insinuations do not make for an efficient restaurant. Whining has never been a treasured attribute of the inspired and passionate.

Steven helps his comrades when needed, and stays out of their way when not needed. He is mostly a pleasure to work with, but gets irritated when under stress. When stress gets overwhelming, Steven will snap and bark his way through the night, demanding favors no matter how unfair they may be, and expecting reciprocity no matter how undeserved. He is not pleasant to work with during his moments of stress, but all in all, Steven is a good guy to have on your team. Never late to work, except when he is, and never showing impatience with even the most challenging of customers. Always sincere, always yielding service with a smile no matter how vengeful the spikes of rage may be.

The Homestead servers are mostly a self-serving bunch, paying mind to the advancement of their own affairs, gossiping of other's, and helping only when it serves their needs or avoids insinuations of their character. Their pay structure calls for them to be so, competing for the largest tip they can inspire from any given customer. Looking out for themselves and their money comes naturally under the system they work for. Occupations are much more than described tasks, they are a reflection of one's childhood bully. Certain ideologies are only natural for certain jobs and corresponding job descriptions, and how we dealt with bullies becomes a metaphor for the stressful moments of carrying hot food for people we may not like.

Servers tend to focus on individualism, which is an easy path to follow given their occupation and payment structure. Since they are paid according to the customer's discretion in the form of tips, the better the service, the better the pay. Or so they think. Often times customers receive excellent service and still refuse to tip in comparable amounts. But when and if the service was actually exceptional is hard to know. Homestead servers always seem to think their particular service is excessive and superior, even when it is lackluster and dull. Boring and sloppy.

Never are they tipped enough, except in the rare case they are tipped too much. When tipped excessively they arise images of being messiah material, claiming themselves the sole reason for inspiring a customer above and beyond normal tipping behavior. When they inspire a customer to tip excessively, its occurrence is obvious from the giddiness and giggling grown men and women do not often display. It would be quite embarrassing, except for the fact they acquired a large sum of money and made their co-workers jealous. And the inspiration of jealousy is all they really want, anyway.

Servers expect the kitchen to provide food expeditiously and delicious enough to inspire customers to the upper extremes of tipping. Kitchen workers demand reverence for the skill they bring to their honored craft from servers. Many Homestead servers could care less about the preparation intricacies of a dish and the required skill it takes, or the passion behind the quality of ingredients used. Unless, of course, it translates into bigger tips. And the cooks don't care about the business of communication management between customers and servers. Unless, of course, it reiterates reverence for their labor.

Leanna runs back into the kitchen, finding Gary to be the first person she sees. "Gary, can you hand me that ketchup? I need it right away. Why do people insist on condiments? Couldn't they just eat their food dry, the way it's suppose to taste? Must they always need to dress it up into something it's not? Does everything need to taste like sugared tomato paste before it can pass the palate?", Leanna remarked as Gary reached over to hand her the ketchup she requested.

She asked with so much urgency that Gary didn't have time to refuse her request. Not that he would refuse even if she didn't, but it's always nice to have options when someone requests favors. Either way, he didn't mind, and Leanna was already well on her way to delivering the ketchup. It would make no difference what Gary thought of the situation now.

Favors are a major unspoken conflict between Homestead servers because friendly favors are not financially compensated. No financial compensation, but no legitimate reason to deny, either. Favors are a necessary evil, if only to maintain the peace and order of a functioning collective. A necessary evil, and one the servers appreciate having a range of choices prior to compliance. Choices are a source of independence, no matter how inevitable the decision will be, or how limited the choices are.

Homestead servers act with a chip on their shoulder, being educated in a semi-skilled profession and still expecting the dignity they feel is deserved. Which is why they require choices. Why else would they pursue college education? It certainly can't be for enlightenment and value of intellect, because intellect has no immediate financial value. Affording intellect is a triumph because of the obscene amounts of money colleges charge for education. Financial ideology of intellect is a forced conclusion for those who sought education under financial premise. Reading, 'riting, and 'rithmatic are too expensive for their own inherent values without the right to brag about them, without the right to wear them as chips on the shoulder.

Barbara walked back into the kitchen, chewing a celery stick in front of Scott, and making a lot of noise as she did. A thick drop of dairy dip stuck to her lip. Servers are not allowed to have anything on their mouths while serving, as it is an obvious deterrent to effective communication between server and customer. Who wants to see their server masticating?

Barbara has this weird habit of showing off her celery stick to the cooks, if only to prove she enjoys eating something she doesn't particularly like. As if it's suppose to prove a maturity of palate or something. Very strange. She's not suppose to be eating at work, but she does everyday, and gets away with it. Perhaps it's pity for her fear of insinuations. For some reason it is much more difficult for Homestead management to enforce rules with females as it is for males, allowing females leniency over many more disconformities than males. Perhaps this is a case for the sexist division of the courts, but that is strongly doubted. Not much of a case could be made over a celery stick dunked repeatedly in nauseating dairy dip. Is it still celery? Or does it become the condiment?

"I need a sub rice for the filet mignon (chomp, chomp, chomp), and extra lemon for the scampi. Thanks guys (swallow), I love you all dearly. Maybe someday you can come to my house and play. You know, a play date. Celery stick?", Barbara pleasantly offered celery to the cooks, even though there is a plethora of food for cooks to eat at all hours of the day.

Barbara still offered with alacrity, not concerned with the potential for rejection. If a cook was hungry, they would cook themselves something better than a celery stick slathered in thick dairy dip. If they wanted to eat, that is. Which they don't. Most cooks suffer the pains of hunger throughout their entire shift because of a deterrence toward food. Very strange. Very ironic. Kendra pondered taking Barbara up on the offer. Cooks are too busy and overwhelmed to ever cook food for themselves, usually satisfying their hunger with ready made snacks and alcoholic beverages. Nothing like hot dogs and vodka to provide the 8 essential nutrients in a well balanced diet. Or so says the cook's handbook of health.

Scott shouted to the kitchen crew after Barbara swallowed her celery, "We need three scampies, one extra lemon, four filet mignons ... medium, rare, rare, mid-well ... the mid-well sub rice. And where are the appetizers for table 21? Crab cakes and steamed mussels? I'm looking for the apps on table 21."

A poignant way to tell Barbara "I'm busy, leave me alone" and "no, I don't want your celery". She ought to know none of the cooks have time to eat right now, and enticing them with this prospect will only make them irritated. Scott continued shouting orders to Ebbi and Kendra, and Barbara left the kitchen to get a carrot stick. She ran out of tomatoes and cucumbers. She also needed to fill water glasses for her customers, clear dirty plates, and get table 20 another round of drinks. But first she has to make sure nothing is on her mouth, to better facilitate communication and not give any insinuating ideas about her livelihood.

Scott could not be less enchanted with the servers as a whole. Not that he detests them in any particular way, but he lacks a dignified respect for their contribution to the restaurant. Scott realizes the necessity of such an arrangement for the Homestead system to function, but advocates a different appropriation of funds and commendation towards kitchen workers. Scott does not offer much respect towards the vigor of communication liaison, much like people who don't eat chowder in Boston.

The increased level of education most servers possess makes them more agreeable to the public's palate, but more detestable to the kitchen. Especially Scott. Individualist servers only grant respectful reciprocity if it advances their personal situation. Which it does. Sometimes. Which they do. Sometimes. But no need to be excessive. It wouldn't serve their purposes. Scott puts up with them, if only because the system requires him to. Scott's first loyalty is always to the system. Always. Even if it means maddening irritation. Sleepless nights and hot eyeballs.

"Oh man. I need to reorder table 3, and take back table 5. Sorry guys, but I made a boo-boo. I confused two of my tables, and I hope ya'll can recover from my error. A million apologies", Kurt lamented as his frazzled face began to sprout several stress pimples.

Kurt gets very stressed when things don't go as originally planned, looking to others for support through the difficult time. An internalization of stupidity overcomes him, only to be reinforced by his stupidity, making a forehead full of tiny pimples.

"Are you going to stop making mistakes tonight, Kurt, or am I going to have to jab my tongs under your armpit? You know Kurt, grabbing the delicate skin of the armpit is really, really painful, and not something you will enjoy. Trust me. It's in your best interest to stop making mistakes", Scott coyly said to an already reeling Kurt.

Scott is not necessarily an intentionally mean person, but he is the sort to douse a fire in gasoline just to see the eruption. Just to get the nonsense of foreplay over with. As long as he is far enough away from the flames, or visible enough to receive liability, he will gas the flames as many times as needed before becoming bored and doodling circles in the dirt. Doodling is just as entertaining, in a much more sedated way.

"Sorry guys, sorry. I'm really, really sorry. I'll stop making mistakes one of these days, I promise. Just as soon as I get my big fat head out of my butt, and start seeing the world through my eyes instead of my butt. I'm stupid, I know. I ought to know how to avoid mistakes by now. Forgive me, it's all my fault. Please don't hate me. I'm doing the best I can, and trying real hard, honest. I'll be a better person one day, I promise", Kurt always defends himself in vulnerable times through self loathing and sarcastic admission of being a loser. Which may or may not be true, Scott will not argue that point with him. But the routine gets a bit tiresome after a while. Self loathing is so pathetic, and not very entertaining given its self defining terms.

Just as Kurt was finishing up his self-loathing schpeel, Barbara walked in through the door giggling a giddiness about her. She wasn't chomping any carrots, but was snickering carrot bits out from around her mouth, making smacking noises as her tongue went from back to front. Maybe not as entertaining as self loathing, but definitely more annoying. For a service industry specializing in food, eating food by its employees is quite the faux pas. Cooks eat only what is agreeable to empty stomachs, and servers are not suppose to show any sign of ingestion or ingestion's affects. Barbara doesn't seem to care, though, and sees an opportunity to pour salt on Kurt's wound with carrot bits still stuck to her lip.

"Geeze, Kurt. You have one little thing to do, and you screw it up. Can't you do anything right? Communicating can't be that hard, can it? Well, you did fetch me that pen earlier, and I thank you, but we have to concentrate here Kurt. We can't go through life carelessly making avoidable mistakes. There is nothing worse for a man than to have other people think he is lazy, incompetent, or clumsy. Start improving your image, Kurty. Don't let insinuations run wild over your image", Barbara instructed as she smacked another carrot chunk from the back of her mouth.

For Barbara, an insinuation of laziness, incompetency, and clumsiness is the male equivalent to female insinuations of being a prostitute.

Scott continued the barrage on Kurt's character, picking up where Barbara left off. "I know Kurt, I'll save you from your mistakes yet again. What else am I here for? All I have to do is run the kitchen and make sure everything in this restaurant is accurate and efficient. Why not, I can be a server too! Sure, I can take time out of my busy day to help Kurt through his erroneous adventures. This under-educated kid who runs the kitchen can help out the poor college boy. It's all in a day's work", Scott's obvious sarcasm had Barbara laughing. Good thing Kurt had left the kitchen by the time Scott said all those things, otherwise Kurt's feelings would have been hurt.

Kendra and Ebbi chuckled as Scott went on about Kurt and his habit of errors, but no one else in the kitchen could really hear him. Kurt's belittling was privileged to only a select few. Nobody else really wanted to listen, anyway, as they had tasks of their own to accomplish without worrying about problems between the kitchen and wait staff. That problem was for Scott to figure out. It's his job. Leave the rest of us out of it. Doug doesn't ask Scott to toss salad during the shift, and Scott wouldn't ask Doug to coordinate communication between the kitchen and wait staff. Fair is fair.

Ebbi finished plating several orders of food, and had a moment to tell Gary the description of the food he made. "The lamb rack is perfectly caramelized and medium, and the haddock is about as fresh as a piece of fish can get. Your table is going to love the food, because all of it was cooked at the peak of its potential. It doesn't get much better than this", Ebbi crouched down, giving Gary serious eye contact as he described the food.

"Wow, looks great guys. Thank you. Most excellent", as Gary turned his head and started to walk out of the kitchen with his food firmly in hand. Walking past everyone without saying a word, he went straight to his table and dropped off the food. Although Ebbi had described the quality of this particular food, Gary didn't say a word of it to the table beyond normal dialogue.

"And for the lady, haddock". The food Gary served looked just the same as any other dish for all cared, and could have been the same as any other dish for all he could tell.

"Thank you", replied the lady as he set the plate down in front of her. To her, it looked like any other piece of haddock she has eaten. And for all she knew, it was. Little did she know or care, a most passionate cook had prepared her food, and little could her bland and underdeveloped palate taste its culinary artistry.

After serving his food, Gary caught Barbara eating another celery stick. He didn't care about the celery stick, although Barbara's eating does take her attention away from focused work. "You know Barbara, its cool and all when Ebbi starts describing all this great stuff about the food, but I just don't care to know. You know, the fish was swimming just a few moments ago, the vegetables have no pesticides, and the rice was first served to the King of China. Who cares? What does it mean for me? I don't know why he can't just give me the food without all the hoopla. I'm busy. I don't have time to talk about the perfect caramelization of lamb racks. Geeze, he's like that guy who lays hardwood floors in your house and won't let you leave until describing every little detail of how they laid the stupid floor. Umm, yeah, that's why I hired you, to do the job so I wouldn't have to worry about it. Now let's finish it without all the chit-chat", Gary took an offering of carrot stick from Barbara as he finished his speech. He took a bite as he started to gather a setting for table 3, making sure not to hurt his sensitive rear molar on the crunchy carrot.

Barbara had a celery strand stuck between her teeth when she started speaking. Watching it flap can be distracting for the listener. "Yeah, Ebbi does that to me, too. I just nod and say thank you, trying not to show him I really don't care, trying to get out of the kitchen before learning about different agricultural techniques for mounding corn compost. Why would I care? It's not my job to know such things. Customers are going to pay the same amount, and as long as we don't serve cockroaches or rat turds, they will come back in the future. And tip well. Ebbi likes to tell us those sorts of things, and I guess its cute. There are worse things he could do, like spraying hot water on my clean uniform. Stupid dishwashers. I could kill Robert when he does that, even if it was an accident of ricochet", Barbara finished chomping her root vegetable while nodding her head. Getting sprayed with hot water is one of her deepest pet peeves. Just thinking about the insinuations is enough to make her scream.

Gary continued, "at least Scott is in a good mood today. Or, good enough. I can't stand it when he starts on his ideology of being an expediter. Why does he take it so seriously? Reading tickets and firing food is not the LSAT, and nor is it a political statement for all to admire. Just give me my scampi Scott, and I'll be on my way, if, that is, Ebbi doesn't hold me up describing preparation, and how the shrimp were only lightly sautéed for that added flavor of the polluted Bangladeshi sea floor." Gary went to the bar, picking up drinks for table 5. A beer and an iced tea, extra lemon.

Tyson put the drinks down assertively, as he has gotten very busy at the bar. He did not have time to chit-chat with the servers about Ebbi and Scott, and nor did he have time to dillydally mixing drinks. When the bar gets busy, Tyson has to work as fast as his hands, feet, and ears will carry him. Running back and forth, mixing drinks, and listening to the difficult conversation of bar patrons makes life an obstacle to overcome. Bar patrons can carry some of the most difficult conversations known to humanity, talking in tones and speaking with intoxicated breath. Slurred speech is never easy to hear, especially when muffled by loud noises a bar is known to have.

Not only do the bartenders provide bar patrons with drinks and conversation, but they also provide the dining room with drinks. A bartender is like an expediter, server, cook, and conversationalist all rolled into one. Except their gateway unlocks a warehouse full of alcoholic drinks instead of food. When people need their alcohol, they can turn into ravenous monsters. Alcohol expediters perform on a different level than food expediters, because alcohol is more a luxury than food, more an addiction than a necessity. People need food, people crave alcohol. For that reason, bartenders are given much more leeway to charge excessive amounts of money for their product, as well as the authority to deny people access to their warehouse when they deem fit. Starving for food is tragic, starving for alcohol pathetic.

Tyson began to yell at the wait staff, "pick up your drinks, and move 'em on out! I don't have time to watch ice marinating into watered down warm drinks, so take 'em out to your customers. Splashed some alcohol in a glass, mixed it with flavor, and now it's time to move. Don't let me see melted ice. I got more important things to do. Keeping up with conversations here at the bar is difficult enough, don't make me deliver your drinks as well. Let's go, take these drinks to your thirsty tables."

Tyson can get a bit nippy when he is under the stress of serving drinks and maintaining conversations across the bar. Wallace seems to be preoccupied with something other than business priority, and that makes Tyson even more impatient. Tyson's impatience is understandable, but not pleasant to be around. Nobody likes to have words shouted at them from a squirrelly looking debaucherist. But being the circumstances as they are, this is the situation servers have to deal with. And truth be told, although Tyson is by far one of the most difficult people to work alongside with, he does mix drinks fast and expedite labor efficiently. And these qualities are treasured by the wait staff above and beyond any character flaw he may possess.

Tyson cannot stand still for long, dancing his way across the bar mixing and slinging drinks. The servers came to pick up their drink orders after the humorous scolding by Tyson, reluctantly completing another job task demanded by the addiction riddled bartender. Tyson had not given them a choice like they would have ultimately appreciated. Most of the Homestead's profit is made from alcohol sales. Servers are told to push drink sales, the wine list is more important than any catch of the day. Perhaps it's the marinated cherries keeping this situation as so. A higher willingness of the people to pay for a drink than food, a deeper willingness to satiate cravings before need, being more enchanted with a shiny cherry than a dull portabella.

There is a stronger sense of independence in consuming alcohol than food, like a teenager tasting alcohol for the first time in defiance of their parents. Self mutilation is one of the most immature forms of defiance, and ought to fade as growth continues into adulthood. But so often it doesn't. There is a strong dependence in alcoholics, as no alcoholic has ever claimed to receive freedom from their addiction. Addictions are dependence, addictions block freedom's future potential. Addictions perpetuate the unhealthiness known to kill a human spirit well before the flesh has returned to earth.

Barbara dropped her pen again, except this time no one was around to fetch it for her. She contemplated waiting for someone to come by before fetching it herself, but because her butt would be seen by all when bent over, she hesitated. Never would she give anyone insinuating ideas about her livelihood. The female butt has been known to inspire the lusts of sexual desire. It was a precarious situation she found herself in, having things to do and not having the time to wait for help to arrive. And yet the fear of insinuating ideas was powerful enough to make her hesitate amidst pressing immediacy.

Because women's labor has, for so long, been confined to notions of prostitution, seeing a woman work outside the home might insight such insinuations. Women's access to future potential has alleviated much of this image in American culture, returning dignity to the labor of women outside of marriage and motherhood. Men had protected their women from labor outside the home for centuries, not allowing dignified females to be seen as prostitutes, no matter how far from prostitution the labor may have been. Female labor had been confined to marriage and motherhood for so long a duration, and social norms do not change rapidly over just one era of time. Or a pen. Or people like Barbara.

Without any more time to spare, Barbara bent over to pick up the pen. Her butt advertised to the world she was a woman available for labor. Namely, prostitution. As she arose from her squatted position, she chomped on a carrot to relax her anxiety, and put the pen in her hair. Gary walked behind her as she rose, and made a comment about the filet mignon being over cooked.

Not paying attention to Barbara or her journey to the floor to fetch a pen, he walked by without taking notice to any issue of Barbara's fear. And perhaps this is the greatest compliment of America's future potential. The dignity of pursuing labor without the demoralizing perceptions of prostitution. To pursue labor and not be forced to deal with attacks of character. To take prostitution away from social norms, relieving slavery from extraneous forces, and returning dignity to its rightful owner. The human being.

Chicken Paste

Removing a gooey mound of chicken paste from its plastic container, Ebbi incorporates processed chicken flavor into boiling water. Chicken paste is used to make chicken flavored broth, a cheating shortcut in the restaurant business to make a stock that would otherwise be a lengthy process. The flavor is not nearly as rich, but ignorant palates know no difference. A restaurant is only as passionate as its customers, and if customers let the kitchen get away with chicken paste, restaurants will take advantage.

Fresh stock is made from a chicken carcass and dry bones, boiled in water for several hours with other vegetables including onions, celery, and carrot-tops. Chicken paste comes from processed by-products of industrialized chicken factories. Not even the chickens are sure which parts of them create the paste. It's thick and sticky, colored yellow, and smells like the bottom corner of the kitchen no one wants to clean. But it goes into our food supply and served to well paying customers. No need to hassle with the labor intensive fresh stock, instant satisfaction is accomplished with three heaping tablespoons of processed chicken paste. Chicken paste makes the chef happy, labor easier, and customers comfortable with familiar flavors.

Ebbi makes and produces his own fresh stock at home for his family, but talent remains untapped in the Homestead kitchen. He portions the stock into individual containers so he and his family can enjoy the rich indulgence of fresh stock whenever they please. Not eating chicken very often, Ebbi usually makes the stock in large quantities when he has the opportunity, throwing in the peels and butts of discarded vegetables.

Chicken paste allows Ebbi to perform many more tasks in a smaller amount of time in the Homestead kitchen. Or something. Fresh stock really doesn't take much more labor time than paste product, is not very difficult, and uses discarded food products in efficient methods. But it does require more skill, and a change in the routine of kitchen procedure. Once an entire collection of people get started in one direction, it becomes very difficult to change their course, no matter how worthy the advice, or how practical the common sense.

Many customers this evening will send their complements back to the kitchen praising the splendid chicken soup made from chicken paste. Ebbi will be hailed as the maker of fantastic soup. Gregg will accept these compliments as fortuitous commendations. Ebbi is compliant with orders from his chef to follow procedure. Even if chicken paste is gross. Deviating from an authority figure is not the path Ebbi is prone to take, having respect and piety for his chef.

"Ebbi, we need you to prepare the red pepper aioli. The recipe is on top of the pastry shelf, but make sure to triple the recipe and use two less eggs than it calls for. I forgot to write it down on the list, but you can start while your chicken soup is coming together", Gregg informed Ebbi.

"Yes, I know where the recipe book is, but I don't need it. I've made this recipe thousands of times. I recite it in my sleep. I know the recipe book better then the recipe book itself. Of course, I would use fresh roasted peppers and not the canned products we use, but who am I to say. I'm just here to follow the orders of my chef", Ebbi replied to a busy chef.

Gregg was running around doing his work, and not paying attention to what Ebbi said. Gregg had given Ebbi the orders, and for all intensive purposes, the conversation ended. Gregg was busy and did not feel the need to speak with Ebbi any longer when numerous priorities trumped the conversation.

"Scott, make sure the carrots are julienne and not coined like last time. I don't want to see any coins going out of this kitchen", Gregg instructed Scott on the preparation of carrots.

Ebbi has become familiar with Gregg's selective deafness, and does not try to change his familiar ways. Ebbi walked over to the pastry shelf and picked up the recipe book, turning to the red pepper aioli instructions. He did not need to look at this recipe, but doing so would satisfy Gregg. Gregg didn't want any mistakes to be made by his cooks, did not want them to take the privilege without written guidance. Mistakes are made when persons are unguided in bureaucracy, as the system upholds routine to thwart mistakes before they occur, even when the routine has become as familiar as walking. Consistency and efficiency. Profits and market expansion. Maintaining happy constituency.

"Make sure you use two less eggs than the recipe calls for", Gregg repeated as he scurried passed Ebbi with a clipboard firmly in hand.

"Two less eggs. I know. And if we run out of eggs we use prepared mayonnaise. And if we run out of lemons we use reconstituted lemon juice. The recipes and substitutions are lodged in my head, chef. There is no need to be repetitive. Perhaps I can ask if you know the recipes as well as I? Perhaps I ought to inquire of your compliance to the structured system? Do you know the system as well as your workers?", Ebbi spoke as Gregg left the vicinity, turning a deaf ear to Ebbi's speech.

"The box of prosciuto is on the back shelf of the walk-in. When you slice it, make sure it is paper thin. I want it to be translucent", Gregg barked at Kendra as trounced away to grab the prosciuto.

Ebbi spoke to himself, "I really believe, with a bit of dedication and commitment, this kitchen could arise as a beacon of inspiration. With a dedication to disciplined food philosophy, and faith in our customer base, we could be the proprietors of fresh food and passion unlike any restaurant confined to normalcy. Our potential would be limitless to the depths of consciousness", as he cracked the eggs needed to make aioli. His words fell upon deaf ears.

The freshness of food poses a dilemma for the food production industry. The fresher the food, the more flavor it will possess. However, fresh food spoils very quickly, and its flavor can be too overwhelming for most customers to comfortably enjoy. A dangerous game of flavor and food cost. A restaurant cannot serve optimal fresh food unless all systems are aligned. Establishing this environment is difficult and does not necessarily imply a financially successful outcome.

When left out too long, fresh food begins to rot, restaurant business systems begin to spoil, and fresh ideas are suppressed without recognition. Once a vegetable is picked, once a fish is taken from the water, once a bread has been removed from the oven, the flavor begins to disintegrate with each passing moment. Fresh food ought to be eaten immediately, or preserved with dignity. Undignified preservatives, artificial ingredients, pesticides, dyes, and chemical washes attempt to prevent this eroding. Reducing the spirit of food into economic products reduces the nutrition potential of ingested food. A homegrown carrot is just not the same as a carrot product stripped of its dignity.

Not knowing how mustard is made, not understanding the moody emotions of rising bread, not aware of emulsification technique. Not caring how an animal was raised for meat consumption, nor wondering how scientists make the preserving substances for food products. Apathy takes a dominant role in our attitude toward food. With an apathetic connection to the food we ingest, the delicate and essential spirit in the food is lost, and we are left ingesting a product void of spirit and full of economic value. Humans were not meant to eat money, but this routine has become all too familiar in our era of culture.

"I don't wash my own laundry anymore. Who needs it? I just drop off my dirty clothes at the corner laundromat, and they do it for me. Cleaned, ironed, and folded without the hassle. What a country we live in, avoiding hassles for a small amount of money", Wendy said in response to Doug's complaint about washing his own clothes. She continued to drain the anchovies.

"This aioli may be the best batch I have ever made. The texture is just right and the peppers were incorporated the way they are suppose to be. Just the right amount of salt, and the perfect amount of lemon juice", Ebbi pointed out his success as he licked his finger clean of aioli.

Having done a splendid job on the aioli, he could not contain his excitement. Unfortunately, his words have yet again fallen on deaf ears. The recipe had been performed to the best of its potential, and Ebbi would make no further comment.

Ebbi holds his critical voice because the workplace is not the proper location to do so. Bureaucracy can be a very lonely place when criticism is afoot. If passions were encouraged at the Homestead, there is no limit to the future potential Ebbi could inspire. Restaurants who serve fresh food are more than mere businesses of food products, they are a collection of pooled human labor to serve people in a community. Centers of passion are few and far between, but when they establish themselves, can inspire the world.

To inspire a chef like Gregg, one must be passionate and patient. Inspiration can be difficult given the realities of dominating influences. Given the conventional truths of a human made fire and the shadows it casts; turning heads to the sunlight can be as painful to the masses as it is challenging to inspire. Especially when shadowed people are good and decent people. Good and decent people simply adhere to the etiquette of civil society. Gregg has the plight of society and practical reality on his side, Ebbi merely a passionate heart and vegetables to tend. Gregg is a good person, Ebbi passionate. Ebbi reads memorized recipes.

Magazine Clippings

Stranger Advised
by Evan Frojo

Dexter Hamlin, now officially presiding as a fully endowed adult, is set to embark on the his first voyage of newfound adulthood. Three days ago he turned 18, and two days ago he bought his first pack of cigarettes. He only smoked one and gave the rest away. Didn't want health to suffer on account of initiation rite. Health lasts much longer.

Tall, strong, and moderately handsome, Dexter reigns from a moderate family of moderate income. A family of kind, considerate, and sometimes loving people, they are a family priding themselves on impeccable oral hygiene. Vital organs do not last forever, but enamel resists the maggots of time.

Dull pearly white teeth are abound in the Hamlin household, without a single denture or cracked crown to discuss between them.

Throughout his 18 year and three day tenure on this planet, Dexter has not a single small filling in any of his teeth. The beauty of his mastication tools shine through every first glance, last glance, and photographic image he smiles for.

Mom, Dad, and two sisters have one cavity and two fillings between them all. Younger sister possesses 2/3 of these infractions. Had to get off a cola and lollipop addiction. None of the Hamlins spew foul or offensive breath, and visits to the dentist are half the recommended yearly frequency. By far, the Hamlins have conquered the challenge of oral health.

Strangely, upon venture to the Hamlin bathroom, one will find five separate toothbrushes but no tube of toothpaste. No toothpaste, and no mouthwash anywhere to be found. No dental floss. Just five toothbrushes and a faucet of running water.

Tonight happens to be a very special evening in the Hamlin household. It's Dexter's final family meal before heading off to college. Emotion filled and stoically anticipated, the family held back hindered tears and an impatience to ingest the warm food in front of them.

Dinner was served at six o'clock. Jasmine rice. Broiled tuna, garlic and ginger. Steamed veggies on the side, mostly consisting of broccoli. Some random carrots. Fruit for dessert, water for beverage. Kitchen scents were abound. Time to eat.

Before the indulgence of this anti-emaciation feast, dad received several inspirational words into his head. He had several glasses of wine prior to seating himself at the large round family dinner table. He cleared his throat.

**Glimpse into the eye of practical thought
You will find reality as its root,
Wisdom as its realm**

**Glimpse into the eye of wisdom
You will find distorted thought as its beginning,
Confusion as its outcome**

The family paused for a moment before eating. Dad sat down and conversation danced lightly around the table. The evening eventually came to an end.

Dexter arrived at his freshmen dorm the next day, introducing himself to Billy, his new roommate. Nice boy; combed hair and pleasant manners made him easy to categorize. A bit vulgar, though. Very shiny metallic teeth. Silver and gold caps, fillings and cavities, shadow stains from braces. Didn't like to smile much, seemed insecure about his mouth. Billy was very well dressed.

As the two interviewed each other for their friendship, Dexter became a slight bit hungry and reached for a carrot stick. He did so carefully, so as not to disrupt Billy's soliloquy on video games of simulated murder.

Billy noticed the carrot stick amidst his speech, and laughed at Dexter's preposterous snack of choice. Vegetables always required bribery for Billy to eat at home. Never would he do it on his own accord. Why would he? Billy pulled out a bag of heavily salted deep fried snacks to satisfy his craving.

Billy and Dexter inevitably outstretched their social skills to include the other new students of their dorm. They rounded each other up after a short period of conversation to attend dinner as a group of comrades. Dining with friends is much more preferable than dining in solitary confinement.

Dexter arrived at the cafeteria accompanied by his newfound friends, only to accentuate his disappointment of food choices. His stomach turned and churned at the sight and smell of the inedible food products to choose from. Strangely enough, his new chums were enthusiastic on the depth and scope of this fascinating menu. Cheeseburgers, cheese fries, cheese pizza, macaroni & cheese, and even sloppy joe's with cheese. Which is funny because this was the first day of college, so how could meatloaf been served yesterday?

The power of social groups and personal insecurity had overcome Dexter on his premier day of college, and he hastily ordered a food

item from the nice lady with a hair net. No
need for heresy amidst first impressions.

At the rectangular table sat Willy, a nice
boy with shiny rows of exquisite metal in his
mouth; Bobby, a taller boy with a sparkling
gold mouth of caps and crowns; Sally, a girl
with a mouthful of well performed fillings and
a beautiful retainer causing her to lisp ever
so slightly; and Billy, now feasting on a
chili dog with cheese and carbonated caffeined
soft drink. Reprocessed meat atop reprocessed
meat and cheese, washed down with addictive
sugar water.

All of Dexter's friends had the finest
doctors perform their dental procedures, never
letting any inferior practitioners get in the
way of oral health. When the light from the
window hit their teeth at just the right
angle, Dexter had to squint from the
reflection of illuminating light harvested in
their mouths.

The dinner conversation had come to an
end, and Dexter stood up to bus his own tray.
No need to finish a frozen chicken patty
anyway, even if it was deep fried. Not paying
good attention, with a sense of uneasiness in
his stomach, he bumped into a strange older
boy near the trash can. Forcefully making this
poor chap drop an empty container on the
floor, it could have been messy had the
container been full. The strange older boy
did not seem angered, as he realized Dexter
had intended no ill intent. The strange older
boy began to speak.

> **If one is not within the realm,**
> **Recognize another who is.**
> **For within the another,**
> **Practical thought is its root.**

Dexter threw away his garbage and caught
up with his new friends. He gave the strange

older boy one last look, as he turned around
and walked in the other direction.

Arriving back at the freshmen dorm, Dexter
began to feel at home. The food was
repugnant, but his pillow was familiar. Billy,
Bobby, Willy, and Sally had bonded rather
tightly over the last several hours. They had
eased each other's pain of recent ostracism
from their families, though they claimed
happiness to be their initial reaction.
"Freedom", they said. "No more rules for an
acquiesce existence".

After continuing conversation, a general
consensus decided it was time for sleep. The
newfound friends journeyed to the bathroom for
their nightly ritualized habits of bedtime
preparation.

Amidst the conversation in front of the
bathroom mirrors, Dexter pulled out his
toothbrush and ran it under water. He then
placed the brush in his mouth and began to
scrub.

"You can use some of my toothpaste. It's
no problem. Accept it as a gift," offered
Billy quite politely.

"No thank you. I don't use toothpaste. I
never have. My teeth are cleaned with just a
brush and water," replied Dexter.

"What? You don't use toothpaste? I have
never heard of anything so absurd," came the
laughing chorus response from Billy, Bobby,
Willy, and Sally. They all took attention to
this unfolding character flaw and continued:

"You must be kidding. Please tell us you
mean it as a joke." None of them could
comprehend this absurd trait of their newfound
friend. Laughing with open mouths, they
exposed the brilliant shininess throughout
their oral cavity.

"Why … do … I … need to? I have never
been instructed to do so by my parents," came
a puzzled response from Dexter.

"Of course! Who doesn't use toothpaste?
Who would ever think to defy convention in
such a way? Don't you want to be healthy?"
Sally was the most disturbed of all four
offended.

"I ... I've never used toothpaste before.
I've never had a problem with oral hygiene. I
don't even have any cavities. Am I doing
something wrong?" Dexter now becoming
embarrassed and self-critical.

"How else do you get teeth clean! Look,
it says right here:"

"FIGHTS CAVITIES" ... "CLINICALLY PROVEN
TO WHITEN TEETH" ... "WITH BAKING SODA" ...
"PREVENTS GINGIVITIS FORMING BACTERIA AND
PREMATURE TOOTH DECAY" ... You see? It all
makes sense. Why would a toothpaste
corporation want to lie? And why else would
legitimate dentists agree?"

Sally and Bobby seemed even more appalled
at the unmasking of Dexter's unusual habit
than Willy and Bobby. All were stunned. Never
had they encountered such strangeness, never
could they anticipate such anomaly.
Dexter placed a dime sized dollop of
toothpaste on his toothbrush. The light from
the hallway hit the mouths of Billy, Bobby,
Willy, and Sally. The bright luminescence was
blinding to Dexter's eyes. He put his hand
above his forehead to shield an attack of
light from the blinding decay of four
unhealthy mouths. All attention in the room
was focused on Dexter. With a deep breath and
a twitch of his nose, Dexter finally raised

the toothpasted brush to his pearly dull white
teeth ... and began to clean them.

Sycophant, My Sycophant

yes, yes, yes, yes, yes, yes, yes, yes, yes, yes, yes, yes, yes, yes, yes, yes,
oh no can't, oh no can't, oh no can't, oh no can't, oh no can't, oh no can't,
couldn't agree more, couldn't agree more, couldn't agree more, couldn't
won'tcan't work, won'tcan't work, won'tcan't work, won'tcan't work,

Oh sycophant! My dear sycophant!
What has inspired your mind to
dismal discourse?
Where can you turn for solace
When your mind tires
And resources exhaust?
A lonesome confinement,
a sycophant's spirit;
Never leaning too far,
Never straying too low.
A life devoted convention.
Wise are those above,
Foolish are those below;
A stressful sleep of infinite anxiety.
May he live to tell the tale,
Of a life without cause;
Perhaps the next
Will learn the lessons past,
Before another sleepless night
May infect a human heart
Who seeks a life to sycophant!

Finishing Begin: The Race
by Hugh Gruffly

Rules and Descriptions:
The race which will ensue henceforth, will
be a race involving characteristics of human
experience. A race not measuring trivial
comparisons of physical speed, skill,
endurance, or strength. A race not containing
intertwined bias of favoritism, favor, or
favorite. A race of human characteristics not
so distant from the daily doings familiar to
many and most ordinary people. Players as
vicarious spectators, spectators as vicarious
players, each involving the other as metaphor.
    The players in this race will be two young
females, both somewhere between the ages of
knowing everything and nothing about life.
Two young females caught between the wide
space of time so often called transition, and
so little called ignorance. Transition from
adolescence to middle-age is a wide space of
time, open largely to undefined space,
interpreting a history of childhood and
predicting a path of future potential.
    The players see the race activities as
mere ordinary happenings in mere ordinary
lives. Nothing special. Nothing dramatic.
Ordinary activities are nothing to be proud
of.
    Ordinary activities are simply part of who
they are and what they do for no particular
reason. The activities of this race are not
activities needing to be practiced strenuously
like a special skill belonging to a gifted
athlete. Ordinary activities flowing so
freely it hardly feels like any skill at all.
    The race between these two young women
will begin in the seventh aisle of the local
grocery store, nuts and candy. Two delicious
snacks in a time of lull between meals.

The two young women involved in this race
do not know the acquaintance of one another.
They live two separate lives, on separate time
schedules, in two completely separate sections
of town. Completely unaware of each other.
Their personalities are completely opposite.
Their order of priorities are nothing the
same.

The time of this race will be sometime
during the week, sometime in the early
evening. The two women will start this race
after a long day of running errands, making
appointments, and satisfying deadlines.

The race is about to begin. It's getting
closer and closer to the starting line with
every passing second. The two young women are
swiftly approaching the seventh aisle of the
local grocery store, nuts and candy. The
excitement and tension is building henceforth,
anticipating the big event.

The Players: *Saunders*

Saunders is a young women, aged somewhere
between knowing nothing and everything about
life. It has become hard to tell her exact
age, as ages tend to blend after a certain
point. It's irrelevant and confusing to pin
down exact numeric ages of people, anyway. So
why bother.

Saunders does not own a personal
transportation vehicle, never finding use for
its advantages and hardships. She does not
feel the need, nor the urgency to embark on
such a personal endeavor of technology. She
feels it will only be so long before our
society realizes it can ill afford to provide
personal transportation vehicles (ptv's) to
every citizen. Ptv's are a very consuming
endeavor. The time and energy Saunders would
put into acquiring a ptv does not equivocate
into a higher level of saved time from its
use.

In defiance of technological methods of
transport, Saunders prefers walking. Most all
people she knows invest their time, energy,
and money into ptv's. Saunders is content
amongst the slower transports of an
industrialized society. Feet. As long as
someone is willing to walk, they can never be
truly stranded. Society always has well
placed checkpoints of civilization, be it a
telecommunication device or public
transportation depot, usually well within
walking distance. Especially within the city
limits Saunders rarely wonders from.
Wilderness does not exist in her life. And
therefore she has never developed a fear of
it. No need to be scared of something that
does not exist.

Saunders wonders if owning a ptv would
make life faster and more accessible, or
simply more confusing. Where does she need to
go so fast? Why does everything have to be so
urgent? What do people wind up doing with
their saved time? And why does it seem people
with ptv's can never get anywhere fast enough?

Although Saunders does not venture into
the treachery of ptv ownership and the high
monetary commitment it requires, money does
not stay long in her pocket. One would think
without the massive financial cost of owning a
ptv, she could save plenty of money. But not
Saunders. Always in the hole, always paying
bill and debt collectors later than required.
Not a month goes by without paying at least
half her earnings to bill and debt collectors.
Bill and debt collectors collecting interest
on bills and debts she owes. Bill and credit
collectors collecting interest on products
Saunders barely even knew she needed. Or what
those products were used for.

However, bill and credit collectors are
rarely able to catch the elusive Saunders.
Bill and credit collectors know where she is,
but can never acquire their full reparation

from her.   She runs too fast from financial
predators to ever be caught in their grips.
Being hunted by financial predators is a harsh
reality for Saunders.   Something she cannot
escape. Saunders runs away when immediate
predators are near, and her life has become
paranoid to their omnipresence.

Easy to find, difficult to catch.

Most all Saunders' product purchases are
with money she does not have.   Credit
purchases made on ensuing debt cost her
several times over the marketed price for
goods and services.   For any article, item,
tool, or service she buys, Saunders pays more
than its actual cost.   More than what it was
worth.   Saunders makes purchases through
credit collectors, not through herself.   Every
time she gets close to terminating her
involvement with credit and bill collectors,
she does something to make sure they remain.
Saunders keeps to herself as an
introverted person. Feeling scared and
insecure when outside forces threaten her.
Creating a shell of protection around her for
defending any and all attempts to penetrate
her zone of introversion.   Never really able
to break herself free, never really able to
stretch herself away from stuffy confines,
Saunders stays alive under an introverted
shell of protection.   Which happens to be just
the way she likes it.   The shell sits
comfortably atop her comfort.
Saunders often feels ashamed of her
lacking ptv. Ashamed of the failure it
represents in a financially driven society.
So much internalized value is placed in the
success of acquiring products in an
industrialized culture, and the lacking ptv
translates into internalized failure. Perhaps
Saunders internalizes a failure in walking
because it reminds her of loneliness.   The

extended length of time walking requires makes walking difficult at times. Gives her that much more time alone to remember her loneliness. Except when the bill and credit collectors come around looking for her. At least then she is not so lonely.

The Players: *Hurriet*

Hurriet is a young women who has lived in this local town her entire life. She knows everyone and everything there is to know about living here. She can't go as far as three traffic lights before waving hello to one of her many friends or acquaintances. Her entire day is a non-stop greeting of "hello" and "how are you" wherever she goes. The bank, the post office, the corner deli for a free sandwich from her old high school boyfriend. Hurriet rarely finds herself paying for anything she acquires from local merchants, always knowing the people operating businesses in town.

The pride and joy of Hurriet's life is the personal transportation vehicle she purchased some time ago. Many aspects of life are defined through her ptv. The particular ptv she acquired was a bit out of her price range, but credit was authorized and loans were obtained to allow the crucial financial transaction take place. Rarely is Hurriet seen by any of her acquaintances without driving her cherished ptv. No one can expect a lofty social status in and around town without appropriate presentation.

Hurriet confronts with much dismay, the credit and bill collectors who seem to follow her throughout the day. They are few and far between, but still a presence to ponder. Confronting, but not yielding any sort of reciprocity to their financial demands. Not afraid to deny them entrance into her personal environment. Hurriet feels an obligation to always confront her adversaries, defending

herself through a strong stance of rigid
obligation. Never run away.

Hurriet feels overwhelmed at times with
her obligations of being who she is. It is
not easy knowing everyone in town. It means
more people to keep happy, more responsibility
to tend. More people to make promises and
favors to. More people knowing the
embarrassing and trying tribulations of her
life. Never really able to experience the
freedom of being an individual. Rules,
regulations, and expectation are all around
her, no matter where she goes or who she sees.

Hurriet is rapidly approaching the
starting line of the race. Seventh aisle at
the local grocery store, nuts and candy.
Hurriet is rapidly approaching everything.
Get everywhere the fastest way possible, the
fastest route possible. Even if quality
suffers, speed is the utmost of importance to
her. Go, go, go. Always doing something,
fending off fears of being lazy. She often
has to battle with these two contradicting
forces inside her head. Run/Lazy. Either she
is going at top speed to accomplish an
infinite amount of needless overwhelming
tasks, or she is down on herself for not doing
enough to feel emotionally satiated. A very
tiring conflict of extremes for anyone to
possess.

Hurriet is currently driving her ptv at
top speed, in effort to get to the seventh
aisle as fast as she possibly can. Nuts and
candy. Which is funny because she doesn't
even know why she wants to get there so fast.
Urgency is just part of her routine.
Regardless of practicality, efficiency, or
reason. Trying to slow her down would be like
trying to touch your right elbow with your
right hand. Of course one must try it at
least once in their life, but quickly
realizing its futility, any further effort is
usually abandoned.

Hurriet is stressing because she's not
getting to the local grocery store as quickly
as possible. Traffic and congestion makes it
hard to travel efficiently. Which is funny
because Hurriet doesn't have anything planned
after the local grocery store. Why hurry? She
may get home to find several messages from
several acquaintances saying she must come and
be with them at a specific immediate
particular time. And then she must go. And
must be thankful she went to the local grocery
store, and her day in general, at the most
optimal top speed. Because if she didn't, she
may have gotten home too late to meet her
acquaintances at the specific immediate
particular time they called for.
Because Hurriet is so focused on getting
places at the fastest speed possible, she
lends herself to the vulnerability of being
attacked. Makes herself an easy target.

Easy target, difficult to penetrate.

Stress. Being surrounded by potential
attackers at all times of the day, everyday.
Seeing any nice person as a potential
attacker. Stressful mind. Seeing nice,
caring, and understanding people as a threat
to your life and livelihood. What a terrible
perception of the world to have. Always being
on edge to protect from all attackers. If
only she didn't have to get everywhere as fast
as she possibly could. If only she didn't
perceive the entire world as a predator on the
heels of attack.

The Starting Line: *Seventh Aisle in the Local
Grocery Store (Nuts and Candy)*
The two young women are inside the local
grocery store as we speak. Each of their
respective daytime journeys has brought them
to this particular juncture in time. One

walking, one driving. They are rummaging
around opposite ends of the store, each in
search of food products to purchase. Product
purchase is an extension of self in a
financially driven society.

Saunders feels she spends too much time in
places she ought not to. On products she
really doesn't need. Bottle of cheap wine. A
loaf of bread and head of broccoli. Saunders
must be mindful of all food products she puts
in her cart. After all, she has to carry
everything home on her back and it's much
easier to be caught by predators when weighted
down with excess baggage.

Hurriet came flying into the store, moving
at a furious pace to get to where she was
going. Apparently, it was the baking supply
section. Wrong turn. Went about the store
pretending she knew exactly where she was
going. Looking up at the directory signs in a
"why do they make this so confusing" sort of
way. Blame it on someone else, the story of
Hurriet's life. She never uses a cart in the
local grocery store. Everything must fit into
both arms at the same time. Hurriet knows
when someone tries to carry too many things at
once in their arms, they will all fall down.
She still refuses to use a cart.

Saunders is slowly making her way through
the local grocery store. She feels the need
to stroll down every single aisle in the
store. She does it more for time than
practicality. She wants to delay the
inevitable. Being home alone. Again. Being
in a store full of strangers is far better
than being alone.

Hurriet has collected several items in her
arms from aisles she's been down. Her arms
are almost completely full, just under maximum
occupancy. She thinks she has everything she
needs. Today, anyway.

Saunders is slowly but surely making her
way through every aisle in the local grocery

store. She has been through the first six
aisles thus far, and has but three items in
her cart. Three not-so-heavy items, mind you.
Except for the wine. The wine is a bit
heavier than the others, but most essential
and well worth the extra effort.
   Hurriet is flying around the store running
like a mad woman in heat. Frantically running
and looking upwards. Upwards to read directory
signs which supposedly help to find what she
looks for. Apparently, they are not doing
their job very well. Hurriet just turned down
aisle number 7, nuts and candy. Still holding
too many items in her arms, looking upwards
and not forward. She's not even sure exactly
what is down aisle number 7, nuts and candy.
But whatever it is, Hurriet will find
something. Something to make it seem like she
knew exactly what she was doing the entire
time.
   Saunders ponders over all the food items
located in aisle 7, nuts and candy. Slowly
moving and gazing, examining all food items
neatly placed along the neatly made shelves.
Her mind is distant and unyielding, thinking
only of the forthcoming evening ahead for her.
The walk home, the bottle of wine. Saunders
normally keeps a full tin of unsalted almonds
on her coffee table, and she just remembered
needs more. Better buy another one. She
picks up a fresh tin of unsalted almonds from
the seventh aisle shelf, turns, and places it
in her cart.
   Hurriet, already pressed for crucial time,
swiftly flounces around the corner of aisle
number seven, nuts and candy.

   **Flouncing and bouncing, announcing her
presently present presence of now. Trumpling
over an outstretched almond arm, crumpling and
dumpling everything in the direction of down.**

What a mess. The collision between the
two young women could be heard at all corners
of the local grocery store, well beyond aisle
number 7, nuts and candy. Not one precious
food item remained in the arms of Hurriet.
All had fallen out of her grips. Trying to
carry too many things at once. What a big
giant mess. Neither one saw it coming.
Saunders, with her head completely turned, was
sedentary and slowly gazing at the food
products available for purchase. Hurriet,
continuing forward with her head tilted
upwards, attempting to read directory signs.
Neither one saw it coming, and neither one
could believe it happened.

The two young women collided in plane view
of everyone in the seventh aisle of the local
grocery store. Nuts and candy. A not so loud
smack could be heard in a radius around the
two young women. An even louder smack could
be heard as numerous food items from the local
grocery store hit the floor. The fresh tin of
unsalted almonds hit the floor first, and then
anything and everything Hurriet was holding in
her overstuffed arms. Packages, bags, glass
and plastic. Everything except the jug of
apple juice. Hurriet was actually able to
juggle the apple juice container for half a
second, trying to catch it before it fell. It
fell. The seventh aisle of the local grocery
store, nuts and candy, was a complete mess.

The two young women looked at each other
with intense and shocked attention. Hurriet
brought her eyes down to look Saunders right
in the eye. Saunders moved her eyes over to
do the same.

The two young women did not look at each
other for very long. The momentary awkward
pause was time long enough. Everything
Hurriet was holding is now on the floor.
Everything Saunders was holding is still in
her cart. Except for the fresh tin of
unsalted almonds. That was on the floor.

Saunders took one more look at Hurriet and
the situation around her. And ran. Leaving
her cart, running away from the messy ordeal
in aisle number 7, nuts and candy. Turned and
ran as fast as she could, removing herself
from all she could not stand to bear. Away
from everything in a split second.

Hurriet watched as Saunders sprinted for
somewhere else, somewhere away from aisle
number seven, nuts and candy. Hurriet could
not help kneel down to pick everything up.
The situation was her fault. No one else to
blame but me. Hurriet even refused the help of
a courteous local grocery store clerk. No one
else ought to suffer for the mistakes she has
made.

After several very slow moments of
cleaning, Hurriet looked toward the exit door.
Saunders was already far away. Removed.
Without the fresh tin of unsalted almonds.
Hurriet remained knelt on the seventh aisle
floor. Obligated. A fresh tin of unsalted
almonds in hand, she slowly put everything
back into place.

Empty Clear

Wallace greets a patron at the bar, an older woman who comes without any companion. The night has been busy for Wallace, but he always puts his business aside to serve his customers even if the stress has been unbearable. His fake smile always seems to fool them.

Wallace: Hello ma'am, good to see you. It is my pleasure in welcoming you to the Homestead lounge, and I will work to the best of my abilities, assuring optimal comfort during your stay. Our lounge welcomes a patron always, in best fun.

Penelope:
Predict preference exposing image.
Image aligned from impression,
Drink metaphoric bridge

Wallace: A tall order, indeed. Most customers order what they wish, without placing so much pressure on the bartender to interpret preferences. I do not wish to associate with customers outside of economic conditions, so if you please, tell me your drink preference. I wish to avoid disclosure foreshadowed, calamity.

Penelope:
Preferences assume fickle visions of the eye.
Economy relation fells amity,
Root expression in clarity (sigh)

Wallace: Ma'am, we are strangers, and for that, our relationship cannot progress past financial exchanges. I do not communicate with strangers who speak in rhythm and rhyme. I cannot speak in jive much less a, jig for dance.

Penelope:
Strangers we may be, siblings we are not, friends we long to hug.
Steadfast and true, surprised I am not, youth ignorance
Beats a drum strings of emaciation tug

Wallace: My emaciation is mine to treasure. Don't take it
away from me, but please, take a drink from my offering. Abundance
of resource to access the Homestead, knows no ration.

Penelope:
Identity radiates unto all who not prostrate.
Former enemies brother this soul to passion
Environment support of foliate

Wallace: I hold an empty glass. It is an empty glass full of
future potential for any drink you prefer to have. Here in this
restaurant we fill empty glasses. Do not disrupt the system, fill your
glass and be on your way to pay. Order now and drink or face
enforced, rent fee.

Penelope:
My friend, I say, who satiates lust.
Very unaware, empty
Desire mistrust

Wallace: I cannot stand here all night with an empty glass in
hand. I have other customers to tend, and hindering their service is
not fair for the money they are expected to pay. Allow our
relationship to go no further, bow to conformity before I lose my
temper. I anomaly loyalty for, no guest.

Penelope:
I be a thwart to system exchange?
It you to hinder progress,
Ignorance lacks change.

Wallace: So I am to change my ways? Am I to change and serve above and beyond normal request? Do you assume me available, whore rotten?

Penelope:
I come as a messenger, purveying
Wisdom easily forgotten,
Seen here without saying

Wallace: What do I see but not speak? How do you wish this empty glass to be filled? Empty glasses are full of future potential, so please, describe how you prefer its filling. Bartender I be but no thought, desire magician.

Penelope:
Tender of needs you are, but no enigma sleuth.
Fire flickers lighting shadow eye's vision,
Caves block sunlight's objective truth

Wallace: Sunlight stings these masked eyes, caves are where I reside in comfort. I will not turn my head to see scintillating pain, I will not twist my neck away from reality. Wine, vodka, rum, tequila or, beer?

Penelope:
Do not rear the neck in twist.
Use vision too clear
Held in fist

Wallace: I hold in my fist an empty glass. I look to it and find no sense. To you, of our situation nothing there but seen, desire.

Penelope:
So clear, so eternal is the glass of potential.
So lost is glass satiated inspire,
Serve clear glass, empty, consequential

Wallace: Your desire is an empty glass? Never have I heard such lunacy across this bar! Yes, by all means, take the empty glass from my fist and treasure it like no other. Have I been blind of this request to, know when dull?

Penelope:
I allow the empty glass to sit afoot
Bestowing radiant potential
Clear, empty, open, no soot

Wallace: I am confused now, whether to charge for your empty request or not. I have a mind to relieve thee of debt, but then our interaction would supercede economic relation. I am not comfortable with such a condition. I cannot endorse discomfort this, spirit fears.

Penelope:
Follow your heart, good man, do what you must.
Enjoy good company, to cheers!
The thwart of system lust

Wallace: Perhaps I will provide the empty glass free of fee. It is not everyday future potential walks through our door. I appreciate your presence much more than financial rewards, thanks from my spirit you, salivated.

Penelope:
I shall remain most empty, yet full
Seated, yet elevated ...

Magazine
Clippings (continued)

Three Bums

By Gregor McGregor, Staff
Columnist

"…so omnipotent man sits back down at the
bar with his brand new one hundred dollar
bill, and orders another drink. And the
bartender says … 'ya know Superman, you can
be a real incubus when you get drunk!"

And off went the gallivant laughing chorus
of vodka stained breath and trivial
patronizing slaps on the back. The three men
had been sitting at the small round table for
an extended time, slurping and gurgling the
night into frolic. They attended this, their
favorite tavern, to unwind after a workday of
stress. Guzzling and gulping high proof
cocktails, they revisit unwelcomed childhood
memories and adolescent moments of awkward
growth with rousing guffaws. Slowly easing
the mental wincing which has gained more
common since their mid-twenties. Why do they
wince? Release. They come for release.

The three men wore loosened neckties and
jacketless shirts around the small wooden
table. The jackets once worn on the men's
backs were tossed aside, as jackets can be
most uncomfortable when worn in the wrong
environment.

The neckties of the three men remained
around three jacketless throats. The neckties
endured. Who knows what glorious substances
would be splashed and drooled atop their pure
silk exterior. Pure silk. Only the most

exquisite of stains will dot their silky
landscape.

Blue Paisley has been meandering fingers
through his hair for some time now, trying to
keep up with the conversation. He has
accomplished five or six twirled knots of
thinning brown strands in the space of three
cocktails. Usually he gets to nine or ten
before deciding to leave.

During sunlight hours, it's unlikely to
find Blue Paisley twirling his hair. This
habit only surfaces at night. There is no time
for twirling when pursuing mundane paperwork
and kissing his wife prior departure and post
arrival of home. And the next kiss is quickly
approaching. Home is on the agenda. He better
drink fast. Sobriety is only a few short
unconscious hours away. Maybe he'll have a
dream tonight.

Blue Paisley, presently approaching six to
seven twirls, halts work on his head when he
notices Polka Dot turning towards him. Polka
Dot constantly adjusts the ball of his left
foot through his leather shoe, and turns
toward Blue Paisley while kicking his own foot
into the floor. It would have been easier to
just take the shoe off. Itches never go away
on their own.

Although varied to constant specifics,
Polka Dot usually fidgets throughout most of
the day. Some of his fidgets are more
noticeable than others, some are quite
personal. Right now he itches the ball of his
left foot without using his fingers. A
daunting task. Earlier, he rehydrated dry
eyes by blinking them harder and more
frequently than normal. Dry eyes can be very
uncomfortable. Hard frequent blinking can be
distracting.

Diagonal Stripes returned to the table
just as Polka Dot had finished the last subtle
kick and press of his left foot. Nobody would
say anything, but everyone noticed the on

going torture of Polka Dot's left foot by its
right-sided counterpart. All were willing to
turn the other cheek rather than acknowledge
the abuse. Neither of Polka Dot's friends
were not willing to confront the issue.

The arrival of Diagonal Stripes from the
bathroom completes the small circle of three
men around a small wooden table. The
conversation picks up to its pre-interrupted
form it had possessed previous to the short
absence of Diagonal Stripes.

Boisterous laughing and admirable
jocularities were sure to ensue in the nearing
moments. Each man had a drink placed in front
of them by their kind server, and each man
looked at the mixed concoction with the urge
to say what was on their mind. None had taken
a sip off the glass just yet. Waiting for
language. Language, the physical expression
of intangible thoughts swimming around the
inner depths of their heads.

Blue Paisley removed the thin red straw
from his glass and slowly lifted his eyes to
conversation level.

"I saw a smelly old bum on the street
today."

The other two men could not help but raise
their own eyes to the level of conversation
Blue Paisley just initiated. Diagonal Stripes
chuckled to himself at the thought Blue
Paisley had decided to share. Polka Dot
slurped a sip of his drink and leaned back in
his chair.

Polka Dot was a bit amazed and sarcastic,
merely replying, "Well, did you say hello?
Certainly, you must have. It would be
extremely rude to not say hello to the man who
chooses your feet, personally, to urinate over
while asking for a few pennies to buy
intoxicants."

Diagonal Stripes laughed without looking
up at the table. He turned his eyes to Polka
Dot,

"Did he ask for financial quotes?
Economic trends in foreign currency? Or did
he ask for some help in getting his diamond
ring appraised?"

"Haw, heh, haw, heh, heh" the laughs were
reflective of the clever joke made by one of
the world's truly finest comedians. Or so he
convinced himself after just a few sips of his
mixed concoction. The other two men looked at
Blue Paisley in an effort for him to explain
the rest of his thought,

"I see this old man on the side of the road. Hadn't bathed in
months.
Dirt tangled his mangled beard, mud crusted his ear.
Fleas danced across his cracked and chattered lips.
Seated along the gutter, kneeling at the foot of despair
Too tired to dance himself
It was not he, as much the flea, in search of elusive feed.

Empty stomach, Empty will.

An old but legible sign hung around his frail neck. Written in
frail words with frail energy.

Struck by unwelcomed
memories.
Never learned society
Vast, confusing…

Emaciated.
Longing for satiation.
Efforts futile
Efforts emaciated.
Emaciated. Mentally emaciated.

"I lowered my head before my brow.
I sped my steps to diligently pass.
Our eyes meet and lay intact,
The downtrodden spirit of a yearning man's heart.

I kept on my way, anxious to say ... not today, not
today."

Polka Dot kept his focus on Blue Paisley,
even though eating peanuts can be very
distracting. These peanuts are de-shelled.
Easier to eat. No shell. No mess. Polka Dot
seemed intent to ask a question. So he did:

"You gave no money? Excellent decision.
They wouldn't fill empty stomachs with nutrition.
Filling their heads with intoxicants. Everyday.
Not deserving to take from society without giving.
They would drink a keg instead of pursuing bread."

Diagonal Stripes was not paying attention.
He ponders a memory of a story he once saw.
He was a child of about eight or nine years.
Eight or nine and a growing boy in a growing
family. He and his family planned a trip to
the metropolis of his home state, and his
cousin had traveled down from the rurals to
partake in the excursion. Diagonal Stripes
never felt comfortable in the metropolis,
always at a weakness outside his home.
The rural cousin of Diagonal Stripes, who
was wearing a sunflower dress, was a mere
twelve years and ten months old. Give or take
a day. Only two months before another annual
celebration of her birth. She was excited.
It's only ten more years until she's twenty-
two and ten months. Give or take a day.
Sunflower Dress resided with her family
amongst farms and farm animals in a rural area
of a moderately populated state. Although her
parents are not actually farmers, she has
attached her identity to the culture of being
one. She enjoys the metropolis for its
contradiction to rural life.
Sunflower Dress entered a subway depot of
the metropolis, seeking to ride a mass transit

vehicle with her family. She was lagging
slightly behind. Diagonal Stripes didn't care.
He forgot she was even there. Most of the
family had forgotten as well.

Forgotten by the family, Sunflower Dress
happened to make eye contact with an old bum.
An old bum with a very old face. Old hands
and old skin. His white thinning hair only
accented the brightest blue eyes Sunflower
Dress had ever seen. And his eyes accented
the most uncombed hair a brush had never
touched.

The old bum hobbled on his limped legs,
somehow able to breathe through the gummy
residue painted on his dirty face. Limping, he
made his way towards Sunflower Dress. No one
in the family noticed the old bum's pursuit.
Closer and closer he came, focused on his
intended destination.

Gummy Residue arrived after his long trek
with a smile. Sunflower Dress smiled and let
out a slight giggle towards the old bum,
turning her head but not her eyes away from
him. Gummy Residue smiled, missing teeth in
full view. A whispering stutter came out of
the old man's mouth. A whispering stutter
with a muffled rasp.

As the whispering stutter finally fell
from his mouth, so did a few strings of sticky
drool. An amiable fist fell from his hand as
an open palm. A palm well withered. And
sticky. He opened his withered and sticky
hand before Sunflower Dress, a hand bearing a
single scuffed and filthy coin. He nodded
towards the coin, motioning for her to put
another on top of it.

Sunflower Dress took an index finger out
of her mouth. She used it to reach for the
coin the old dirty man offered her. Little did
she know this man was not the sort to give
charity, but the type to receive it.

At the moment of midpoint distance between
the index finger of Sunflower Dress and the

dirty hand the old coin was attached to, came
the intervention of the dominant family
female. The watchful eye of Sunflower Dress'
aunt had seen the last half of the interaction
between the two. Immediate intervention was
taken. A yelp, a tug of a twelve year and ten
month old arm, and an entrance onto a mass
transit vehicle ended the altercation.
Sunflower Dress and Gummy Residue would never
meet again.

Diagonal Stripes rendered himself silent
to his friends for the last few moments. He
still remembers the look on her face as she
was being dragged away. No remorse. No fear
of danger. No sense of wrongdoing. No
threats were made upon her life, threats
others assumed to be made. Just a look of
dissatisfaction that contact had not been made
with Gummy Residue. If only she could have
touched him.

Polka Dot interrupted Diagonal Stripe's
blank stare into the corner of the wall with
an interesting tidbit of information. Well,
maybe just interesting to the people seated at
hand. It seems as though Polka Dot was in a
similar situation as Blue Paisley not too long
ago. Walking amid the congestion of the
downtown area, Polka Dot encountered a bum. A
bum seemingly clean aside from his poor oral
hygiene. Aside from poor speaking habits and
offensive breath.

The bum was seated in front of the public
water fountains. Many restaurants and
eateries surround the fountains, and many
people eat their lunch here on warm sunny
days. Polka Dot arrived one hour after
lunchtime, a time when few professionals are
left, and off-peak business travelers make up
the sparse eating population.

Polka Dot was eating off-hours for the
first time in a long while. He had grabbed a
quick sandwich along with a beverage, making
it a lunch on the go. He had shoveled the

first bite of sandwich into his mouth when he
noticed the young man with poor oral hygiene
and offensive breath.

  Polka Dot was not impressed. He described
the situation with a tone of excitement, as if
he was building the story to a point of
comedic climax. His eye contact and body
language suggested the end of the story would
see the young toothless man as the blunt end
of his jocular intentions.

> "Short hair.
> Not shaven.
> Teeth falling out.
> Sat with backpack and cat,
> Gazing eyes, hopeful heart.

  He yelled and sparked at innocent
strangers, Asking for a small but large amount
of money. He caught me as I looked at his
sign. Held in front of body, telled a story,
felled an innocence. Paper cardboard, dark
ink.

I want an Intoxicant.
Give me money for Intoxicants.
Don't like to work,
At least I'm honest??

> "Looking at this man, much dismay,
> I reply to speaking written words.
> 'At least you behold honesty!'
> I flipped him a tip of bit,
> I insist,
> profitable day.
> Before he could mutter
> the thanks I deserved
> He scolded demands for money
> from a lady with stiffened hair. I walked away.
> Amused."

The three gentlemen were slowly
encroaching on the final sips of their
elaborate mixed refreshments. Polka Dot was
still laughing. It was his own story, and he
laughed the loudest of all three men.

The men were not quite ready for the next
round of refreshments. The lack of eye
contact with their server made that abundantly
clear. Blue Paisley leaned into the middle of
the table, elbows resting on either side of
him. He looked intently like he was going to
say something, but didn't. He looked at the
bottom of his glass and just stirred the ice
around. The mood of the night had slowed.

Diagonal Stripes was seated reclined, one
arm slumped over the backrest of the chair.
He had not successfully rid his mind of
Sunflower Dress and Gummy Residue, and the day
of metropolis. Why had he remembered this
story above others? Why would he remember the
facial expression of his cousin at such a time
of adversity? And why was he feeling the
uncontrollable urge to share this story with
the others right now?

Well, he did share the story. From
beginning to end. There it was, a true
childhood memory for his companions to be a
part of. A display of perception and emotion,
insight into the character structure making
Diagonal Stripes into the man he has become.

So there he sat. Diagonal Stripes still
reclined in his chair, making only glimpses of
eye contact when the moment arose.

He told the story and further described
the sign of the old bum. It was a ragged old
sign, but legible nonetheless. Gummy Residue
had left it behind as he approached Sunflower
Dress. Diagonal Stripes saw it while being
thrust into the mass transit vehicle.

The bum had obviously possessed this sign
for quite a while. No piece of tinted glass
could look like that without living a long and

stressful life. The words were written with
dark paint. It read:

Lost within self.
Cannot overcome
Vast unwelcomed
memories. Never acquired
precious sense of society. Too
Individualist.
Could not make use of society.

     The end of the story left the men
speechless and out of energy to prolong the
evening. The night was growing old and solemn
thoughts were abound. They could not
understand how bums could maintain themselves
on a daily routine with their lifestyles.
Everyday. The same thing. Everyday.
     The tab had been sitting on the table for
several minutes now, and attention was turned
to its situation. The men pulled out their
wallets. Enough money was laid down, plus a
tipped bit for the kind server to keep. She
earned it.
     The men stood up and began merging towards
the door, a slow but steady process to
eventually show results. They were finishing
their conversations, with interesting and
irrelevant tidbits of information they could
not squeeze into the night's main discussion.
     Polka Dot was listening, but mostly
staring out the window. His eyes seemed a bit
glossy. He was not fully involved with
Diagonal Stripe and Blue Paisley's chatting.
Listening, but not involved. Just enjoying
his adventures of eye wandering.
     The gentlemen greeted the kind server one
last time before leaving the establishment.
Diagonal Stripes turned around to catch her
attention before they had left. She was happy
they had thought of her, making an intent to
bid farewell for an evening well spent. She
stood against the bar, waving goodbye with one

hand and holding onto a menu with the other.
The gentlemen saw the menu, but didn't need to
read it.   They already knew what it said.

    Bread .... $money
    Water .... $money
    Vegetables .... $money
    Fruit .... $money
    Meat .... $money
    Intoxicants .... $money
    Place To Share Discussions .... $money
    Social Contacts .... $money
    Service By a Willing Person ... $money
    Smiles from a Server .... $money
    Society Runs Business .... $money
    How Society Thrives into
    its Future Potential ... Inspired Passion

    The gentlemen tipped their hats as they
exited.   They were happy to have come, and
happy to depart just the same.   A tall glass
of water was waiting for the three men at each
of their respective homes, a glass of water
used as antidote for the sickness of
dehydration.   The sickness looming for
tomorrow morning.   Being sick is not fun or
admirable.   Better to be healthy.   Better to
be well hydrated.   A dehydrated person cannot
function effectively from day to day.   And the
men need to function effectively.   They would
like to come back tomorrow.   And the day
after.   Everyday.   Hydrated.

Sergeant Pepper For the Ages

by: Shell Fargus, Staff Columnist

I can remember it quite clearly. I was walking to a friend's house with a six pack of beer in hand, avoiding puddles on this rainy night and pondering worldly thoughts of life, liberty, and the pursuit of happiness. As I hopped over a small puddle on this cold, rainy night, a tear streamed down the side of my face mid-jump and mid-thought. A true tear, not a misinterpreted stray raindrop. As I landed across the puddle, many tears began to stream down my face. I'm not the crying type, and it took several tears to realize I was, in fact, crying.

So there I stand, beer in hand, motionless and crying on the other side of a puddle on a cold rainy night. The crying did not last very long, maybe 25 seconds, but the impact of this enormous moment of realization has lasted a lifetime.

Moments of realization do not come along every day, and actually, many people are lucky to have just one in their entire lives. Especially over thoughts that are not suppose to have tremendous effects on people. Family, society, philosophy, life, and the cosmos are all acceptable realizations for someone to have. But The Beatles?

All my life I have heard older generations talk about The Beatles and how important they were to American culture. As a person born well after their final breakup, many aspects of my understanding escape me concerning The Beatles.

Yes, I can look at footage from the concert at Shea Stadium and see how popular this band was. And yes, I can go out and watch their anthology videos and see even more

footage proving their unmatched popularity.
And yes, I do own most of The Beatles' albums
and listen to them frequently. But many
questions have been left unanswered in my
pursuit of understanding what John, Paul,
George, and Ringo meant to society in 1968.
What was their message? Why were they here?
And why do they continue to be one of
history's great historical characters? Many
of these questions remain unanswered for
future generations to interpret. Finally, the
future generation is here.

I began to be suspicious of my
understanding of The Beatles when a very
simple question could not render any tangible
answer from even the most devoted Beatles
fans. All my life I have been listening to
Sergeant Pepper's Lonely Hearts Club Band.
"The first concept album", I heard. "A
milestone in music", I was told. "Nothing
like it, pure genius", people agreed. So in
the midst of such genius, why couldn't anybody
answer some very simple questions? Who is
Sergeant Pepper, and why do we care? Who
exactly belongs to this Lonely Hearts Club
Band? And what exactly is the "concept" in
this first "concept album"?

Asking a Beatles fan these questions
returns futile results. A blank stare, and a
pompous, self-righteous look is your answer.
Basically, they don't know. But they do
accomplish making you feel stupid, as they say
in a round about way, "you just don't get it
because you're not as enlightened as me." And
then they'll throw the old Grateful Dead line
in your face, "if you have to ask, you just
don't get it."

Basically, they don't know the answer but
are too afraid to admit it. But they don't
want anyone else to know they don't know the
answer because everyone is suppose to know the
answer. And if you don't know the answer,
just make everyone think you know it. Give

'em the old Grateful Dead line, that will shut them up and make you look smart.

But I did ask. And I wanted some answers.

Asking Beatles fans was futile, they didn't know. Searching music references was futile, they didn't know. Hearing other answers never seemed right. Watching the Anthologies wasn't going to say. Listening to the album was pointless, the answers are covered and mysterious. So the answer to my simple questions was going to take a little more than your average means of research. I did not expect the kind of effort it was going to take, nor did I realize The Beatles were so philosophically deep. But they are. Like I said, I'm not the crying type.

Answers started to fall in place when considering Paul McCartney's supposed death sometime in the 1960's. Rumors at the time were flying around that Paul was in fact dead, and the band tried to cover up his death because of the hysteria sure to ensue if this was true. The Beatles were so popular at the time, that the death of Paul McCartney would cause riots and hysteria throughout the world. The conspiracy theorists believed Paul had died, and was replaced by a similar looking man without any one being the wiser. Playing records backwards, analyzing album art, and interpreting certain lyrics hinted towards this theory to be true. And of course it wasn't … well, kind of.

Paul McCartney was not physically dead, nor was he ever physically dead in the 1960's. But the idea that Paul may have been *artistically* dead is relevant. After all, the 60's were the era of new expanded thoughts, and more relevantly to Paul's artistic death, the Grateful Dead and the spirituality of death ideology. Artistic and spiritual death was a new thought at the time, and the concept

of being artistically dead had meanings
stretching far beyond the definition of not
being physically alive.

Artistic death meant creating great ideas,
being in a place of great enlightenment, and
performing at a level second to none.
Basically, hovering above everyone else on a
heightened plane of thought. The mid to late
60's was this sort of time for Paul McCartney,
and he played around with the ideas of
artistic death in his works. Hence, the clues
found throughout albums and writings, and the
scare of Beatle fans everywhere when they
thought this could be true.

The idea of Paul being dead and replaced
by a similar looking man is the main concept
behind the "concept" of the Sergeant Pepper
album. Literally, The Beatles were asking
their audience, "what if Paul had died and was
replaced by a similar looking man? Would you
care? Would it matter?"

So the question is asked, who is Sergeant
Pepper's Lonely Hearts Club Band?

Sergeant Pepper's Lonely Hearts Club Band
is not so much a person as it is a concept of
people. Sergeant Pepper's Lonely Hearts Club
Band is the group of people and inanimate
objects that influence our lives, but whom we
do not have tangible relationships with.
Basically, idol worship. As the cover art of
the Sergeant Pepper album may suggest as
examples: Albert Einstein, Sonny Liston, Bob
Dylan, Karl Marx, a television set, Edgar
Allen Poe, Gandhi, Marilyn Monroe, and of
course, The Beatles themselves. All of these
pop-culture idols are part of Sergeant
Pepper's Lonely Heart's Club Band.

The concept behind Sergeant Pepper's
Lonely Hearts Club Band is the understanding
and separation of two different kinds of
relationships we have in our lives: tangible
and idol.

In contrast to the idol relationships we acquire through Sergeant Pepper's Lonely Hearts Club Band, our tangible relationships include family, friends, and members of our community. People you can touch, taste, feel, and smell. People who directly influence us in everyday life. Not idol characters and images as we see in Sergeant Pepper images, but real people. Mothers, fathers, sisters, brothers, grandparents, best friends, worst friends, enemies, co-employees, husbands, wives, etc.

So the question is asked of the Sergeant Pepper concept: say someone like your father is replaced by a similar looking man with similar character traits. *Would you notice*? *Would you care*? *Would it make a difference*? Of course it would. Because your father is a tangible relationship irreplaceable by another. But if someone in Sergeant Pepper was replaced by another similar looking character, like Paul McCartney with Billy Shears, it would not matter. *Why*? Because Paul McCartney is not a tangible relationship to his millions of fans who only know him as an idol.

If Billy Shears was able to perform at the same level as Paul McCartney, it would make no difference that he was not the authentic McCartney. We can replace him because he is only a character, only an image in the Lonely Hearts Club Band.

The Beatles were making a distinction between these two sorts of relationships in their concept album. The Beatles were also pointing out the dangers of confusing these two relationships as obsessively as many of their fans had done. Many Beatle fans had made the confused mistake of blending these two different types of relationships without any distinction. All the lonely, confused people who had mistakenly blended the image they had of The Beatles with their tangible relationships.

Thinking John was their father, Paul their boyfriend, Ringo their buddy, or George their brother. The Beatles, no matter how much the fans would confuse, were never tangible to their fans. The Beatles were images on a TV set, a photograph, or sounds on a recorded album. They are members of Sergeant Pepper's Lonely Hearts Club Band.

And so the album goes. The Beatles were analyzing tangible and idol relationships. Sergeant Pepper's Lonely Hearts Club Band encompasses all famous and infamous figures of history, life, and pop culture. The Beatles had taken a critical dig at their own fans.

The Lonely Hearts Club Band is the image of themselves they put on stage, musicians who learned to play from previous Sergeant Pepper artists, the musicians who played the instruments on the album. The Beatles did not play any music on the album, it was the Lonely Hearts Club Band that did. Musicians who look similar, play similar, and sound similar to The Beatles. But they're not The Beatles, they are The Lonely Hearts Club Band. *Why are they not The Beatles*? Because unlike tangible relationships, it does not matter who the people are, it only matters who the characters are.

The album's songs consistently alternate between the two relationships from the beginning to the end of the album. Each song describes an aspect of each relationship with alternating precision. A song of idol worship, followed by a song of tangible relationship, followed by a song of idol worship, followed by a song of tangible relationship; etc. There is an objective break in the middle with *Within You Without You*, where the song philosophically speaks of how to obtain a better understanding of life, the album, and ourselves.

A listing of the songs and their alternating pattern:

Track #1: (Idol Worship) "Sgt. Pepper's Lonely Hearts Club Band"

The opening lyrics of the title track reiterate the influence of Sergeant Pepper relationships on The Beatles:

"it was twenty years ago today,
when Sergeant Pepper taught the band to play"

When The Beatles made this album in the late 60's, The Beatles were in their late twenties. Twenty years before would put them all in an age range of 4-8 years old, when they started to play instruments as influenced by Sergeant Pepper culture. The Beatles are quick to acknowledge the old American blues records they listened to at these ages, as well as a wealth of different movies they watched. The American blues musicians were part of their Sergeant Pepper, as The Beatles were influenced but had no tangible relationship with them. These people, among other Sergeant Pepper characters influencing The Beatles, taught the boys how to initially play their instruments.

The song continues with the idea that the performers on stage are the unimportant impostors of The Beatles. Billy Shears is the singer, not Paul McCartney, and the audience loves it. Why? Because Billy Shears sounds exactly like Paul McCartney. And of course, the Lonely Hearts Club Band sounds just like The Beatles and wants to take the audience home with them, but they cannot. Why? Because they have no tangible relationship with them.

Track #2: (Tangible Relationship) "With a Little Help From My Friends"

The next song, in alternating pattern from the previous, is one of tangible relationships, speaking to the tangibility of friendship. Friends wouldn't walk out on him if he sung out of tune, while the audience of a Sergeant Pepper relationship would. But not with friends. Friends are tangible, friends are lasting, friends don't go away when times get out of tune.

"How do I fell by the end of the day?
Are you sad because you're on your own?
No, I get by with a little help from my friends"

His relationship to his friends keep him company at the end of the day, something Beatles fans could not do.

Track #3: (Idol Worship) "Lucy in The Sky With Diamonds"

This is a song which has been under a lot of controversy since its release. This song describes obsessive fans of The Beatles, and not psychedelic drugs as many people have assumed. The song tells of experiences concerning the fanatical fans following the band everywhere they went. The girl with kaleidoscope eyes is a female fan constantly appearing throughout their lives, never leaving them alone, always mesmerized by their image. Literally, invading their every thought and dream in life. The girl with kaleidoscope eyes does not understand the difference between tangible and Sergeant Pepper relationships, following The Beatles wherever they go attempting to make tangible what cannot be. She is a very confused person, and her behavior terrorizes their thoughts and dreams.

"picture yourself on a train in a station, with plasticine porters with looking glass ties, suddenly someone is there at the turnstile, the girl with kaleidoscope eyes"

Track #4: (Tangible Relationship) "Getting Better"
     This song is of tangible relationships with the self. A song taking us from childhood to adolescence, and then into young adulthood. The essence of the song is that change and growth comes from the tangible relationship to oneself and the tangible experiences of life.

   "man I was mean, but I'm changing my scene, and I'm doing the best that I can"

Track #5: (Idol Worship) "Fixing a Hole"
     Here The Beatles are questioning themselves as authority figures. The song is asking, *how can you* (the audience) *believe our every word*? *How did we get put in this room atop everyone else, where whatever we say is correct*? *And why can nobody manage to get past the door to this room of authority except us*? *How has this become reality*? *Why did the audience puts us here*?

   "and it really doesn't matter. If I'm wrong I'm right, Where I belong I'm right"

     The Beatles are really asking their fans to take a look at the reality that has become Beatlmania in *Fixing a Hole*. This song also says how silly the fans have become with their obsession of The Beatles, and how The Beatles deal with the stress.

Track #6: (Tangible Relationship) "She's Leaving Home"
     Mother, Father, Daughter. It highlights some of the troubles this family has in their tangible relationships with each other, over their daughter leaving home. But where is she going? Maybe to follow The Beatles, maybe to follow some other Sergeant Pepper. Either way, in *She's Leaving Home*, the parents are

very upset and trying to realize the error of
their ways.

"Standing alone at the top of the stairs, she
breaks down and cries to her husband, Daddy,
our baby's gone"

Track #7: (Idol Worship) "Being for the Benefit of Mr. Kite"

Sergeant Pepper relationships toward
politics. As many performers and actors are
part of Sergeant Pepper, so too are most of
our politics and political leaders. Mr. Kite
is a political leader who is leading the
procession of political rhetoric. Politics can
be a very damaging source of idol
relationship, especially when people falsely
believe they are part of the political
process. The song is deliberately confusing,
as it symbolizes the bureaucracy and rhetoric
of politics.

"Messrs. K. and H. assure the public their
production will be
second to none.
And of course Henry the Horse dances the
waltz!"

Henry the Horse is part of the pomp and
show of politicians to manipulate and distract
people.

Track #8: (Philosophic break in the album) "Within You Without You"

This song directly describes the concept
of the album. The "space between" is the
confusion of knowing which relationship is
which, and the answers to life's greatest
mysteries are always within you.

"we were talking - about the space between us
all, and the people - who hide themselves
behind a wall of illusions."

Track #9: (Tangible Relationship) "When I'm Sixty-Four"

A tangible song about love, life, and family. *When I'm Sixty Four* speaks of the aging processes of life, family, and marriage.

"will you still need me, will you still feed
me, when I'm sixty four."

Track #10: (Idol Worship) "Lovely Rita"

Rita is not necessarily an actual meter maid. Rather, the Lovely Rita is a female member of Sergeant Pepper who is used as a fantasy sex object. The "meter" is the coin-operational aspect of fantasy sex objects. The song is about the fantasy sex figures in the media and our minds, and the connection we feel for them. The song speaks to the many people who have sexual relationships with fantasized sex objects, and questions the fantasy's healthiness. The panting and breathing at the end of the song are symbolic of the masturbation associated with envying these fantasized sex objects. Masturbation to a Sergeant Pepper figure is part of the general confusion pointed out in the album.

"Lovely Rita meter maid,
where would I be without you,
give us a wink and make me think of you."

Track #11: (Tangible Relationship) "Good Morning, Good Morning"

Once again, The Beatles keep to form. The alternating pattern between idol and tangible relationships continues with *Good Morning, Good Morning*, where Lennon speaks of the more mundane aspects of everyday tangible life. Being in a home town, seeing the same people, realizing that nothing changes too drastically in the course of a lifetime. Tangible relationships aren't without criticism from

The Beatles, as this song exemplifies a depiction of everyday life.

"Then you decide to walk by the old school.
Nothing had changed it's still the same,
I've got nothing to say but it's ok
Good Morning, Good Morning"

Track #12: (Idol Worship) "Sergeant Pepper's Lonely Hearts Club Band (reprise)"
The band on the album (which is not The Beatles, just a band that looks and sounds exactly like them) says their farewells, leading into the final track of the album.

Track#13: (Dual) "A Day In The Life"
This mystifying and enchanting song keeps to the form of the album all within itself. It is able to blend both aspects of tangible and idol relationships into one, complex song. The song begins by speaking of the Sergeant Pepper relationship people have to media, with news he's heard through films and newspapers. He describes stories he has acknowledged through media sources, only to be cut into by a rendition of tangible life and everyday activities. After finishing the rendition of everyday life, the song returns to the Sergeant Pepper relationship one has to the media. Both idol and tangible relationships in Sergeant Pepper's Lonely Hearts Club Band were fused into one for this final track.

"I saw a film today, oh boy.
The English army had just won the war" ...

"Woke up, fell out of bed
Dragged a comb across my head"

As I stopped playing the album over in my head checking for mistakes, I realized I had found the answers I was looking for. The Beatles had made sense to me on this cold,

rainy night. My own life had made more sense
to me on this cold, rainy night. I directed
the question The Beatles had asked back to
myself: *Can I separate the tangible and
Sergeant Pepper relationships in my own life?*

Like I mentioned before, I am not the
crying type. But when concepts as large,
intricate, and relevant as The Beatles' album
of 1968 hit your head all at once, the
response can be a little overwhelming.
Especially when I am not expecting them on my
way to a friend's house with a six pack of
beer in hand.

Although I hadn't conceived much of it
before, The Beatles were able to describe an
aspect of my life I was not previously aware
of. The realization of a large, intricate,
and relevant concepts of life can never be
predicted. Nor could the tears be stopped as
I hopped over a puddle. *Why do some people
feel closer to their intangible relationships
than their tangible ones? How has this become
prevalent in our culture? Is it reflective of
a capitalist political economy*?

Before arriving at my friend's house, I
dried both my eyes and gave my head a good
hard shake. I cleared my mind of all Sergeant
Pepper concepts, so as not to distract the
evening at hand. I walked into my friend's
house, said my hellos, sat down, cracked open
a beer, and began talking about the local
sports team. They're just going to have to
wait. But hopefully not forever.

Dialectic Conversations: Retention & Expulsion

Antiphia: Ebbi, I have a desire to ask more questions, for I feel there are deeper understandings of truth I am not conscious of.

Ebbi: Your feelings are correct, as there are deeper understandings of truth we have not spoken of.

Antiphia: I am understanding the truth of both earth and water, but how do they relate to practical wisdom? How do they relate to the practical maintenance of day-to-day life, the paths our lives follow each and every day?

Ebbi: I will begin by explaining how the behavior of earth and water work in practical applications of the human body, animals, plants, and all other creatures. The body transports water around the body, using earth as its guide and foundation; earth is maintained in the body by the flow of water. The more easily and harmoniously the water shall flow, the more grounded and founded the earth shall be, the more healthy the creature will grow.

Antiphia: I still do not fully understand.

Ebbi: Unlike our discussion of the eyeball, we shall now discuss the practical application earth and water play into the relationship of our bodies. We shall now discuss doorways.

Antiphia: Doorways?

Ebbi: A doorway of the body is an aperture between the body and the environment. The mouth, nose, anus, penis, vagina, eyes, skin, and ears are examples of doorways. Some expel, some ingest, some do both, but they are all doorways between the body and the environment.

Antiphia: How do they relate to our discussion?

Ebbi: Doorways are points of potential for either great health or great ailment. Great hydration or great dehydration. When doorways are healthy and vibrant, the body will be healthy and vibrant. If doorways are sickly and abused, the body will be sickly and abused.

Antiphia: How do doorways relate to the body in such a way?

Ebbi: First, I must speak of energy potential. We will use the mouth as our first example to demonstrate this point.

Antiphia: Very well. But why choose the mouth?

Ebbi: The mouth is the easiest human doorway to describe and understand, and will fit our needs nicely to further the discussion. We will use saliva as our example of energy potential in the body, and how it relates to the doorway of our mouth.

Antiphia: I am listening.

Ebbi: Energy potential is the maximum amount of energy every organ of our body aspires to have. The higher the energy in any given organ, the healthier and more vibrant it will be.

Antiphia: Continue.

Ebbi: If a person has a habit of constantly spitting their saliva and expelling precious oral fluid away from their mouth, the saliva duct is forced to work itself to replenish the lost saliva. The saliva duct always wants to maintain its optimal level of saliva for the health of the body, and will work until this optimal level is satiated. If someone constantly spits, the saliva duct will be forced to work endlessly for a satiation it cannot achieve.

Antiphia: And why would the saliva duct be inclined to work in such a way?

Ebbi: Because it does not want to let the other organs suffer on account of its failure. The saliva duct will do all it can to assure the body has an optimal level of saliva for its health.

Antiphia: So the saliva duct is part the body's cosmos, and it will always strive to be at an optimal level of production?

Ebbi: Yes. The optimal level of production cannot be maintained if the mouth has a constant habit of spitting as we have described. The duct will never reach its optimal level as long as the doorway keeps spitting, and will become overworked as it produces more and more saliva without ever reaching its satiation.

Antiphia: So the saliva duct will be overworked because it will continuously seek to produce an adequate amount of saliva it will never attain, because the mouth will be spitting carelessly?

Ebbi: Precisely. When the saliva duct is overworked through a spitting doorway, it will not be able to produce as much saliva, or as high a quality saliva, than if the doorway was opened with more care and respect.

Antiphia: So you are saying we will deter the potential of our saliva duct if we abuse its intentions?

Ebbi: Yes. But now we shall take it one step further. Remember the body is a dynamic entity, and all of its parts are interrelated to one another. We are now inspired to ask, after understanding the isolated characteristics of the saliva duct, what is the dynamic effect of this abuse on the cosmic body?

Antiphia: I would like to hear your answer.

Ebbi: Remember how we concurred that there exists an optimal energy potential, not only for the individual organs, but also for the complete body?

Antiphia: Surely, I remember this.

Ebbi: And would you agree, that all organs of the body feed off each other's energy, and each one is dependent on the others for optimal health?

Antiphia: I wholly agree. But I seek to understand how they communicate with each other, and what is the method of their interrelation? How could this relationship be defined in comprehensible terms?

Ebbi: Remember the movement of water and the earth. The organs communicate with each other through the movement of water throughout the body, from the most insignificant crevice of the body to the most essential. The healthier and more vibrant the flow of water, the healthier and more vibrant the communication, the healthier and more vibrant the body.

Antiphia: Every organ in the body would like to perform to its potential, to provide the body with optimal health, and each organ acts under humility for complete health. The metaphor for this truth is the flow of earth and water.

Ebbi: And this metaphor is governed by the health of doorways.

Antiphia: Yes, I understand this, but I would like further description of doorway dynamics.

Ebbi: Let us refer to the example of saliva duct we have spoken of. When excessive spitting is performed through the doorway of mouth, it places a drain of energy on the saliva duct, because the duct is forced to overwork itself, trying to satiate the body's need for saliva. Every time it produces a drop of saliva, saliva is spit and the duct is forced to produce more. Overworking outside of its means, the duct now must search elsewhere for its lost energy, because it has expended all of its individual energy. Desperate, it begins to search elsewhere for the energy it requires.

Antiphia: Where does it find the energy it needs once its own sources have been depleted?

Ebbi: Needing more energy, it begins to take energy from other organs of the body. The other organs are forced to give their own energy away to aid the struggling saliva duct. The body works as a cosmos, which is why they share energy when needed elsewhere. The saliva duct will drain energy of other organs and subsequently waste it as saliva is spit through a careless open mouth doorway. As each organ begins to sacrifice its energy, blockages in the cosmic flow of water begin to appear, and the foundation of bodily earth is slowly depleted.

Antiphia: Continue.

Ebbi: The other organs begin to suffer as the energy drain becomes larger. As the mouth spits more and more, the saliva duct will take more and more energy away from the other organs, reducing the overall energy level at which the cosmos operates. The body suffers, various ailments appear, health and longevity are disrupted.

Antiphia: I see. The energy drain not only injures individual organs, but the complete body. Unforeseen ailments begin to appear, because organs unattached to the saliva duct begin to suffer as if they were. The spitting doorway has reeked havoc on the cosmos, and the affects are felt throughout.

Ebbi: With an energy drain of the saliva duct, the liver will suffer, the pancreas will suffer, the heart will suffer, the eyes will suffer.

Antiphia: Excessive spitting will injure much more than the individual saliva duct.

Ebbi: Every organ in the body will perform at a lower level of efficiency because they cannot achieve their satiating potential. Each organ will perform at a reduced level of quality and quantity.

Antiphia: I see your point, although I find it hard to believe such a dramatic influence could be had on the body from the saliva duct.

Ebbi: You are correct, but remember the saliva duct was just an example. It does not have as dramatic an effect on the body as other abused doorways.

Hardwood Fried Rice

It's the late morning of an otherwise normal Friday, and Ebbi spends time before work helping his sister lay hardwood floors. Bridgette and her newlywed husband have purchased a home just a couple of months prior, and are in need of new floors. The previous owners of the house had several cats who repeatedly sprayed the carpet with pungent cat spray, creating an odor forcing this particular home improvement. Low on money and unenthusiastic about an odor soaked carpet, Bridgette requested Ebbi's help. Ebbi is handy around the house, and even though his hardwood floor experience is lacking, he learns quickly and uses the proper tools for the job. Ron, Bridgette's newlywed husband, helps Ebbi lay floor on the weekends when he is not working.

"Would you like some soup?" Bridgette asked as Ebbi pounded another slat of wood into the hardwood puzzle. Bridgette has taken a break from work to prepare lunch. She works at home filing papers for an accountant, financially supporting her competency and marriage without leaving the house. Hungry, and anticipating her brother's hunger just the same, she made her way to the kitchen with soupy thoughts on her mind. She enjoys having Ebbi at the house, if only to break the silence so often accompanying weekday hours.

"I still have the quart of fish broth you made, frozen in my freezer, waiting for an opportunity to be made into soup. I have several other ingredients we can add, making it a delightful afternoon treat for two hardworking people", Bridgette continued as she looked around the kitchen for all possible ingredients to add.

She looks with urgency, if only to impress her brother the family cook. She wants this to be the best soup she has ever made, even though she knows Ebbi will come into the kitchen and help regardless of how much personal initiative she takes. Which is what she really wants, anyway.

"Soup sounds delicious. I haven't eaten all day. How is your work coming along? How is technology treating you these days? Any complications made by the little elf who lives inside your computer?", Ebbi asked as he pounded yet another slat of hardwood floor. His stomach just started to growl when his sister offered him lunch. If there is one thing Ebbi does not enjoy, it is suffering the pains of an empty stomach. He strategically, and purposely, prepares food for his family to assure good quality nutrition will be available for them. Broths, sauces, condiments, and entire meals are residing in the kitchens, refrigerators, and pantries of all his siblings and two parents. Everyone enjoys Ebbi's food with heartfelt warmth, a gift of passion only a cupboard away from their hearts.

"Technology has been good today. No devious little elf to complain about. A little boring, just going through the motions of an ordinary day. Being a little bored is probably a good thing, no serious stress or conflicts to worry about. After I warm up the broth, do I add the noodles and vegetables? I like the soup you made a couple of weeks ago, the one with spinach in the sweet egg broth. Could we make that again? I think I have some spinach left over from two nights ago", Bridgette explained as she went looking for the spinach.

And with that question, Ebbi stopped his floor work and entered the kitchen. Ebbi knows when it's time to begin important food preparation. Even though Bridgette made the initial effort to make lunch, both of them knew it would only be a matter of time before Ebbi would take over the reigns. Bridgette prefers it this way, smiling as her reliable brother comes to rescue lunch from the mere ordinary. Bridgette always asks questions and inquires about different techniques in Ebbi's culinary repertoire, but when it comes down to it, having Ebbi prepare the food himself is preferable to any other option. Unless, of course, she has the opportunity to prepare the food with him. Ebbi's hands work in a way few can understand, and even fewer can put into actualization. Ebbi's food creates magical moments with each and every stroke of his dancing paintbrush, each and every chew of his delectable food.

"After the broth begins to steam and swirl ever so slightly, incorporate a dollop of mustard with a wire wisp. Add just a touch of salt and a few good turns of ground pepper. Do you still have that fresh pasta I left here last week? I'll start to boil some water. And no, I don't think we can make the sweet egg broth because we don't have aji-mirin. But the mustard fish broth will be just as good, I promise", Ebbi gently instructed as he found a jar of his homemade mustard, a bunch of cilantro, garlic, onions, fennel, spinach, horseradish root, and carrots, all from his garden.

The fresh pasta was in the freezer. He began chopping the cilantro as Bridgette slowly began dicing the onions and peeling the garlic. The preparation of lunch had started, and Bridgette now wore a big smile on her face as she knew Ebbi would soon be serving a soup of immense magnitude. She had gotten Ebbi over to her house to lay hardwood floors, but she could not let him leave without preparing the food she loves to eat.

"The carrots can be sliced on an angle, and the fennel needs to be shaved as thin as you can possibly shave. The thinner the better, if only to accentuate the potential flavor fennel offers. Look at this carrot. I poked the spade fork a little too deep right here, made a small hole when I was digging them out of the ground. The earth was a bit tough that day, and I guess a few carrots got injured during harvest. Its been a good year for carrots though, almost all of them have been coming up without being eaten by furry creatures or crawly critters", Ebbi described his adventures in the garden as he continued to chop cilantro and grate fresh horseradish. The broth was barely warm, still far too early to incorporate the mustard.

After Ebbi finished describing his carrot harvest of the season, Bridgette took a step back from her cutting board and began staring at her knife. Ebbi continued to chop the cilantro. Her eyes began to see the garlic as something more sacred than the mere bulb it had been just moments prior. Ordinary life had just taken a turn towards the sacred. Until this point of the day, Bridgette had been doing ordinary boring tasks in her ordinary boring work room, became hungry, and sought to alleviate her hunger with the culinary help of Ebbi. But now, standing alongside her brother and preparing food in tandem with him, it had become something much more than the ordinary and boring.

Something more spiritual than merely relieving hunger pains. She paused and spoke. "Ebbi, where do you find your passion?"

"Passion? In family, gardening, and cooking. You knew that, though. Why do you ask?", Ebbi responded a little puzzled at Bridgette's inquiry.

"But I have family, gardening, and I know how to cook, but you seem to have a degree of understanding much deeper than anyone else I know. Where does it come from? We share many of the same stories, many of the same friends, and many of the same tribulations expected of two siblings. Why have you acquired a passion of understanding while I struggle to find the spirit within myself? Why don't my actions radiate like yours? How do you look at an onion and see passion, when I only see a mere onion?", Bridgette asked, seeking to understand her brother.

"Metaphor", Ebbi explained as he continued to prepare the cilantro. He chops into small pieces, leaving the small bits of cilantro stem for full flavor and texture.

"Where do you see it though? Where does metaphor exist? How can you be so inspired amongst people who view life as pointless drudgery?", as Bridgette began to slice the onion she now saw differently.

"The metaphor of earth and water exists is in our food. We ingest what our body needs, according to our cycle of health and longevity. The energies of the external world also live inside our internal world. Food is a doorway of potential", as Ebbi moved his knife to the horseradish root.

"Can I add the mustard now? I think the broth is swirling", Bridgette asked.

"Yes, we can add it. I'll wisp the broth while you add the mustard. The flavor of mustard will complement the taste of ocean in the broth, and it will also add a thickness of texture to sooth the tongue and coat the palate. Never forget the importance of texture when creating flavors. Every flavor needs a ground of support to confirm itself as genuine", Ebbi softly directed as his sister began to spoon mustard into the broth. Ebbi's whisking sent the broth into a lively swirl, priming the broth for mustard incorporation. The smell escaping the heated pot brightened the room. A rich, complete smell burroughing its essence in the bridge of their noses.

"Why am I stuck at an uninspiring job? I don't really want what mass culture has made me want. I need the money I make, if only to satisfy my own definitions of success I learned through internalizing economic values. I feel empty, and looking at you, you are so very content with life, a life I have found to be filled with copious amounts of pointless drudgery.

If this be our situations, why does our society favor my position, and largely discredit people in yours? Why do we reward people like me with treasures of money, and allow people like you to live in dearth?", Bridgette emphasized as she split a carrot in half to slice it. Cutting carrots in half prevents it from rolling.

"The dearth American society requires me to have as a result of my lifestyle can be disheartening at times. The job I work does not financially compensate me like a corporate lawyer, my garden does not provide me with a lucrative retirement package, and my devotion to family does not get me free tickets to baseball games. Perhaps one day our society's values will change to meet the future potential of human existence, but until then, I will continue to grow my carrots and remain a happily inspired man", Ebbi spoke as he began a long inhale over the simmering broth now incorporated with mustard. A pleasant smile stretched across his face.

"I never realized you yearned for more money. You hardly have any interest in the material products more money would bring", Bridgette inquired with a bit of hesitation in her voice to hear Ebbi's reply.

"I yearn to feel a part of my society and culture, it's a yearning to seek the actualization of America's future potential, not because I lust after material possessions, but the future potential of our people. I am left to preserve my own competency largely independent of society's help. Although I revel in this independence, it would be nice to have the same support and regard we have for corporate lawyers", Ebbi pondered while thinking further about the future potential of soup.

"Well, at least your job is aligned with your passion. It is commendable that you are able to support yourself with a job highlighting what you love to do. Not many people can make this claim about their lives, having an occupation as an extension of love", Bridgette tried to instill some cheerful words into a more sullen looking Ebbi. She helped him pick the spinach.

"I yearn for passion in my work, Bridgette. Right now, I have none. The restaurant business is designed just like any other business, a center for profit potential to those devoting themselves to currency acquisition required by a financially driven society. The work I do at the Homestead is work based on profit margins and not passion. Food cost and not love. Volume and not spirit. At work I am required to follow recipes and pre-designed routines of proper food preparation, not my own artistic expressions. At work my paintbrush is taken from me and replaced with a calculator. Numbers reign supreme. I am not allowed to stray from regimented guidelines, for fear of repercussions by the chef. I am not allowed to display my passions at work as one would think, even though I am completely capable of doing so. My work at the Homestead is just as replaceable as with any other cook working alongside me. My talents have no tangible relationship to actualization", Ebbi revealed his shortcomings at work as he sprinkled fresh cilantro into the broth.

"Ebbi, I thought you were happy at your job. Why have you never told me of your discontent? You don't get to display your passions at work? But why? You are the most passionate person I know. If they allowed you, the restaurant would flourish beyond all financial comprehension. The food would be unique and spiritually satiating, and people would come just for a taste. I yearn to eat your food if only for these reasons, and I am positive any stranger would travel great distances to have the same opportunity I am given here in my own kitchen. Have you talked to Gregg? Have you made him realize the future potential existing right in front of his face? That an opportunity like you does not come along in every human's life, and you could change the entire world from the Homestead Restaurant? Does he realize the source of a wonderful American renaissance could originate right under his very own shadow?" Bridgette was

now less preoccupied with the soup than she was discussing her
brother's troubles at work.

She is so emotionally attached to her brother's cooking that she
cannot understand how someone else would not want to experience it
for themselves.

"Gregg is a good chef, and one who understands the
groundwork of running a business. I do not want to interfere with his
system or objectives, because the Homestead is very financially
successful. It is difficult to criticize when success is present. I may
not view profit seeking as a virtuous skill, but constituents of the
Homestead do. How do you criticize a successful leader? How do
you criticize a system when that system accomplishes its intended
goals? How do you change the definition of intention? How do you
change the foundation of values and means of acquiring intended
goals?" Ebbi exclaimed as he began to sauté the vegetables on a
medium heat. Bridgette placed the noodles into the boiling salt water.

"It seems as though you would be able to exemplify your
passions if you could show Gregg what kind of unique talents you
posses. Has he ever seen your passions?", Bridgette inquired with a
deep intent to understand her brother's behavior when he is at work.

"No, they never give me a chance. The business objective is
very focused on performing the recipes to an exact instruction, and
performing the system according to its requirements. They don't
have the time or patience for listening to new ideas. They are afraid
to taste my food, they are afraid of the unknown. They do not
understand what passion looks like. They equate the value of food to
economic standards, they readily eat the food products a financial
society provides for them, preferring food with lacking flavor and
high in profit inducing ingredients", Ebbi confessed to his sister as
they watched the cilantro swirl inside the broth. Its flavor was now
part of the soup.

"You need to show them your passions. Following their
recipes and regimented guidelines is no way for you to live. You
understand a higher degree of metaphoric food, and your talents could
be a wonderful asset to them. There is a wealth of understanding in
what you represent, and it is imperative for them as well as yourself

to pursue the expression of these talents," Bridgette emphasized with a slurp of soup from the ladle.

"But I have learned to be content with repressing these talents at work. Work is what it is, and I am not going to make it into something it was not intended to be. Americans want their work environments to revolve around a financial aspect of value, and I have come to accept this truth in our working American lives. It has proven to be successful on its own terms. I go to work to make friends and earn the money necessary to support my competency in society. Nothing more. I use my passions to provide my family and home life with the satiation I long for it to have", Ebbi continued as he indulged in a slurp of soup from the same ladle as his sister, pausing briefly to analyze its flavor for any necessary adjusting.

The pasta water returned to a boil, and the vegetables were crackling under the heat of a sauté pan ready for deglazing. The soup was almost complete. Ebbi allowed the noodles to boil until perfectly al dente, using this time to deglaze the vegetable pan with a mixture of rice vinegar and a dash of water. Allowing the mixture to reduce and absorb into the vegetables, he lightly sprinkled kosher salt and fresh cracked pepper. He pulled the vegetables off the stove, placing them into adequate portions between the two bowls. He drained the noodles through a colander, rinsing them immediately under cold running water, rubbing together to wash off any excess starch. Ebbi then poured a small amount of sesame oil over the noodles, along with a soy reduction sauce he had made previous. He placed an adequate amount of noodles in each bowl atop the vegetables, pouring the mustard/cilantro/fish broth over both, completing the soup. A simple lunch taking less than eleven minutes to prepare, but a lifetime to remember.

"I think all those around you would be enchanted if only given the opportunity to see future potential in the workplace. They might be resistant to change and the unknown, but once a person sees truth they can hardly deny its relevance. Just show them the truth you understand so well, radiate your spirit as you do your family, and they will be sure to notice what a treasure they have in their presence", Bridgette finished before blowing on her soup and diverting the steam every which way.

"I've already discredited work as a viable place for inspired expression to take place. The paintbrush I use at work is dull and stodgy, guided by the bureaucracy of numbers and profits. To dance at work would mean my inevitable termination, if only for the deliberate misuse of a conditional paintbrush. Dancing is a fruitless endeavor given the bureaucratic atmosphere of American business", Ebbi spoke as wafts of steam consumed his face from Bridgette's bowl.

"This is a great tragedy for our bureaucracy, the inability to provide an adequate atmosphere for an inspired person to dance toward future potential. Our society would be much closer to the actualization of future potential if special people like you were able to find their paintbrush in a work environment. I pity the Homestead for not taking advantage of your gifts, and a little disappointed in my brother for not pursuing his own paintbrush. I beg to ask why you have surrendered so readily, when so much potential lies ahead and your spirit lies dormant", Bridgette wanted to know as she took her first sip of soup, inhaling steam as she sucked the broth inward.

"There was a time when I would readily express my passions at work. I wanted to make food as best I could, with every ounce of energy I could muster in every dish I was instructed to prepare. I was working here in Portsmouth, at my first kitchen job, and as a young enthusiastic worker, I wanted to show everyone what I was capable of. I read books seeking more insight into the art of cooking, and I developed culinary techniques with a great interest", Ebbi mentioned as he sipped his first sip of soup, inhaling the omnipresent steam of the room.

"And this is where you learned the talents of cooking? I do not remember our mother or father teaching you to cook during childhood, and I can only assume your talents came from the job you acquired while still an adolescent. Did you find your passion in a bureaucratic work environment?", Bridgette added before inhaling more steam.

"Yes, this is where I first learned the art of cooking. I worked very hard at this job, and learned all I could from the available information given to me by the chef and my coworkers. I excelled at this job not only because I learned how to be a successful worker, but how I could enrich my talents", Ebbi described.

"And you continued to make food according to your instruction? When did you break off from the regiment and begin to create your own path of culinary artistry? When did you start deciphering ingredients and implementing a deeper philosophy in food preparation?", Bridgette inquired as a spoonful of broth and carrots entered her mouth.

"Everyone must first acquire inspiration before dancing down a new path", Ebbi spoke as an onion hit his tongue.

"When was the day you were finally able to dance down that path? What inspired you to pursue passion?", Bridgette now ate a spoonful of carrot, onion, fennel, and steam together as one.

"It was not until one day when Allan, a good friend and older co-worker, asked me if I had ever taken my talents home with me. He asked if I use my talents to impress my family, to make home cooked meals many American families never experience. I thought about his question for a minute or two, and simply replied that I hadn't. Allan told me my talents developed at work would be worthless if I did not bring them home, because I was young and the money I was making didn't matter anyway. His words meant a lot to me, and they are words I have always remembered," Ebbi said as he put his spoon down to inhale more steamy broth.

"So the bureaucracy taught your talents of inspiration? Having never realized your passion or talents at home, you found them in a work environment? And now you say the same bureaucratic environment that supported these talents is preventing you from future potential? Are you making any sense?", Bridgette exclaimed as she looked at her brother for his reaction.

"Yes, I am making sense. The bureaucracy was able to initiate my talents, but it eventually left me where I could not pursue my path. Many people have experienced this in bureaucratic culture, and have called it the glass ceiling. This is why I have chosen to pursue my passions at home, where I have the freedom to express myself without bureaucratic hindrance," Ebbi replied amidst a mouthful of steaming noodles.

"What made you think you hit the glass ceiling? Was there any specific incident to convince you?", Bridgette asked. She dotted her face with a paper towel.

"I was at home, pondering Allan's advice, and I decided to make dinner for the family. Neither mom nor dad was home, and I wanted to make this a surprise for all to enjoy. Mom and dad never liked having me in the kitchen, always telling me this or that, what I could do and what I couldn't. Mother never enjoyed my company in the kitchen, as she found it to be a room of great stress and a garrote of frustration. I had always loved the flavor of fried rice, and decided to make a large batch for the family to enjoy," Ebbi reflected into his soup.

"Fried rice? When you were still an adolescent? I don't much remember this moment, much less remember eating your fried rice. Was I home? Did I eat it? How did it turn out?," Bridgette swallowed her spoon of soup as she enthusiastically asked questions.

"Horrible. Absolutely horrible. By far the worse dish I ever made. Transferring my talents from work into the home were more challenging than I had assumed. I did not realize fried rice was made with previously steamed rice, and not the raw rice I used straight out of the bag. I heated up a pan with vegetable oil, and dumped two cups of raw rice into the smoking hot pan. The smoke and fumes arising from the pan were horrendous, and every inch of the house stunk like burning starch. I did not even get to add the broccoli when I realized soy sauce burns and becomes a gooey mess when heated. There I was, standing in front of burning raw fried rice being held together by a goo of disgusting soy sauce, and smoking the house into suffocation. I brought the hot pan over to the sink for washing. As soon as I put the pan under the cold water, it splattered and hissed at me something awful as the pan began to warp. Just as soon as the warping started, mom walked in the door. Horrified by the horrendous smell and choking smoke, she ended my fiasco with one good disconcerted look in the eye", Ebbi laughed as he remembered the facial expression of his mother as he pieced together the details of the night.

"What did they say? I'm sorry for laughing, but this story is very funny. Why have I never heard it before? Did she scold you?

Was she upset? How did she react?," Bridgette inquired with a sense of urgency.

"Yes, she was upset. And too confused to laugh. Asking what I had done, and why I had done it. Why the house smelled like it was on fire, why I wasted two good cups of rice, why I warped the pan, and why the rice stuck to the pan like glue. 'We'll never get this off' mom said as she let out disgruntled moans of disbelief at my errors of the evening. The pan had been destroyed. She wondered why I had not left the cooking to her, as I had always done throughout my childhood. She wanted to know what prompted me to break from routine, but I just couldn't tell her," Ebbi remarked as he continued to eat his soup and steam. A cilantro flake had gotten caught in his teeth.

"Mom was upset? How did she scold you?", Bridgette asked.

"She told me to leave the kitchen, to put the pan in the garbage, and not to waste good food ever again. She did not want my help in cleaning the mess I made, preferring to accept the burden of my errors on her shoulder. It frightened me from pursuing my talents for some time to come. It struck a serious blow to the confidence I developed," Ebbi responded with a happiness in his breath.

"But why would this incident allow for you to become passionate at home, and not at work? If I understand your story correctly, you would have ran back to the restaurant eagerly yearning for that satiating environment, away from great failure at home", Bridgette tried to understand before eating more noodles and steam.

"When pursuing passion, we will often stumble at first before we hone our talents. Much like a new born horse stumbles as it takes its first steps before being able to gallop, a cook will burn fried rice before coordinating large and intricate meals", Ebbi slurped more soup with a smile on his face.

"But you did not stop there. You stumbled, but you continued to pursue your talents until they have become as divine as they are today. I don't understand, Ebbi. If you relate the bureaucracy with your home experience, it seems as though you have completely reversed their influence. You developed talents at work, not at home. You stumbled at home, and did not stumble at work. If you became frightened at this stumbling, why did you pursue your passions at home and leave the passions at work dormant and apathetic? Why are you complacent to hit the glass ceiling at work and not at home?," Bridgette was now determined to know. She put down her spoon just to show how urgently she wanted to know the answer.

"The bureaucracy does not allow you to stumble. They never provide the opportunity to fail in a miserable way. If I had been able to stumble at work, I would have been better able to pursue my passions. The fried rice failure was my first dance with a paintbrush. The Homestead cannot let me stumble, and therefore I do not have the opportunity for passions to succeed," Ebbi lamented through a smile of content.

"And you were allowed to stumble at home," Bridgette pondered while nodding her head up and down.

"Mother was upset, but I had that important opportunity to fail with my first dance. I had the opportunity to fix my mistake and try again. The Homestead would never give me an opportunity to fail, much less another opportunity if I did indeed fail at work with a horrendous burning odor," confessed Ebbi as he lapped up more of the broth.

"Then I am glad we were able to let you stumble, because your talents have blossomed into the fine dance they have become," Bridgette recognized.

"Cheers"

And the two clasped their spoons together and finished lunch for the day.

Bureaucracy of Future Potential

As the evening shift came to a close and customers began whittling down to a dubious few, the kitchen crew began cleaning the night's mess. Food preparation can be quite messy, and sanitation is necessary for any kitchen's survival. Wiping, mopping, scrubbing, sweeping, and shining to a glossy perfection what once was riddled with spills and splatters. Unclean kitchens have been known to be sticky, foul smelling, corrosive, and bait for unwanted critters to crawl themselves into feast. Cleanup is quite important, involving all muscles of the body to maintain sanitation and discipline. Backaches are not uncommon, groans, moans, and creaking ankles are expected but worth the price. Cleaning is essential to the cook's job, if only to keep unwanted critters out of the bounty and a smile on the chef's face.

Although any chef would be adamant about routine kitchen cleanup, the chef is a constant absentee from it. As executive of the kitchen, the chef is excluded from the creaking ankles of sweeping floors. Nobody wants to see a chef toiling in the scummy grit of a crusty underbelly. Nobody wants to see a leader in vulnerable positions. Weakness might give subordinates ideas of insubordination. During cleanup, Gregg usually escorts himself to the chef's office where he has a small drink of whiskey, reads a magazine, and on certain occasions, smokes a cigar and sucks down raw oysters. Although he hasn't smoked a cigar in quite some time, or shot an oyster for that matter, the moment can strike at any time. Kendra saw him take a bottle of cocktail sauce. A not so unspicy cocktail sauce. Slurping an oyster as he exhales smoky mist, relaxing after a tiring shift. Contrasting tangy cocktail sauce with sharp whiskey, the smoke of the cigar clears his palate for another oyster.

As sous-chef, it is Wendy's job to supervise cleanup efforts. Gregg has delegated this important responsibility to his most trustworthy comrade, confident all will be well by night's end. Wendy usually offers a hand to aid subordinates of the less grueling tasks, but most often remains true to her clipboard and management position. Most of the physical labor is left to the cooks and dishwashers. Her central task is to take inventory of all products, avoiding the unpleasant inefficiency of having too many or too few food products. Ignorance towards inventory could mean the demise of a restaurant, as it is a most critical component in an efficiently functioning system. Wendy is a critical link of efficiency and profit at the Homestead, and never would she want to be so naked in front of people who matter most. She takes her job very seriously.

"We need another carrot cake for tomorrow. We sold nearly all tonight. And we'll need more chocolate sauce and raspberries", Simone informed Wendy of her inventory needs. Wendy made a note of it on her clipboard and thanked Simone for the valuable information. Wendy picked up a tray of fruit for garnishing desert plates. Missing were the raspberries, empty was the chocolate sauce, sparse was the carrot cake.

"Hey guys, there's a customer out here who wants to order some food. I know we're closed, but is there anything we can make for her? She's really hungry. What do you say? Can we make her something to eat?", Wallace asked as the kitchen crew moaned and groaned with each strenuous wipe of sticky grease.

"Nope. Sorry, kitchen's closed. She missed us by about twenty minutes, but we'll certainly be open tomorrow if she wants to come back. We can't turn on the equipment again, as you can see, because its laying on the floor and being scrubbed. No can do, amigo", Scott replied to a disgruntled Wallace. Wallace hoped to please the customer as best he could. It failed. No more nourishing food available, only the intoxication of alcoholic beverages.

And so it goes. Another night of business completed in the Homestead kitchen, another night of serving public emaciation avoidance has come to close. Tired and anticipating the completion of a work shift, they hang on for just a few more moments to push through the last wave of responsibility. Scott put a lock on the refrigerator door, a lock symbolizing terminated access to all food products. The distribution system is closed and food is unavailable. Unless they paid an exorbitant amount of money, or sought access approval from a qualified authority figure. Otherwise, even the most destitute and emaciated human would be left to rot in spite of the luscious foods stowed in the Homestead kitchen. Until tomorrow. Distribution systems are just as important as the food itself. Without food, people starve. Without efficient food distribution systems, people starve. And without an expediter to mind the gateway for system compliance, people starve. Mold the expediter, support the system, status quo obedience. Bureaucracy.

Ebbi cleaned his sauté station as he does every shift, using cleanup time not only as a means of pest control, but as a moment of meditation in his busy day. A moment to take a deep breath and focus on his thoughts without distractions of serving emaciation avoidance. Many cooks do not enjoy cleaning after a long shift of cooking. It's the grit after glamour. Ebbi could not bask in the warmth of raving food complements if he was not willing to get his elbows dirty in grittiness. Many cooks see cleaning as beneath their dignity of skills, and ought to be appropriated to a lower ranking kitchen employee. Clean areas are known deterrents of critters, foul odors, food decay, sickness, and cross contamination. What is lesser known of gritty cleanup is the foundation it lays for future potential to sprout forth.

"Where have you been putting the white wine bottles? Have you been putting them on the top shelf above the oven? They're suppose to be on the back wall, right where I can locate them in a pinch. The bottles are worthless if I can't find them when needed", Ebbi said to a squatting Scott. Scott was in the middle of wiping out the lower cooler, a job forcing a stretch of the arm to its lengthiest potential, and inspiring a grimace on the face of a squatting expediter.

"What?", Scott replied in a stretch to reach wet cheese droppings. The cheese stuck to the bottom of the cooler and smeared itself, making Scott's life that much more grimace filled.

"The white wine. Where have you been putting the white wine? It goes on the back wall, not on the shelf above the oven", Ebbi repeated in a slightly louder voice.

"Yeah, the back wall. That's where I put it. Why? Do you want it on top of the oven?", came the shouts of Scott, wet rag hanging from his right hand dripping chunks of smeared cheese.

"No. I thought you were putting it on the top shelf. If it wasn't you, it was someone else. Don't worry I'll find out who it was", Ebbi said with a vengeful look in his eye and a chuckle on his lips. He knew how serious kitchen work was and how serious it could be, but also knew not to take the urgencies of system dynamics too dramatically. Incorrectly placed white wine bottles were annoying, but it did not entail a battle between line-cooks.

Amidst the scramble of a kitchen in sanitation work, Ebbi found time to munch a sandwich he made for himself. Simone sealed up the last of the cakes and pies, Doug put a wet paper towel over the lettuce, Kendra put fresh ice on the fresh fish, Scott wiped all the counters, and Robert started to spray the stack of dirty kitchen tools handed to him in heaping mounds. All were stretching for the finish line to close the shift on a sanitary note. All were stretching for the finish line except for Ebbi, who now took a moment to lean against the counter and focus his attention on the sandwich. Tomato, avocado, and lettuce on baguette bread brushed with basil infused garlic olive oil, sprinkled with salt n' pepper, and toasted on the grill. A perfect way to end another night of business at the Homestead.

Although Ebbi completes all his work in timely fashion, leaning does not bode well with the chef. Especially when Ebbi is also eating away food cost. But given the night as it went, and given that Ebbi does not have any time for a sandwich prior, it is understandable to eat and lean as the shift winds to a close. After all, Ebbi is an important teammate on this kitchen team, and his cleanup work has progressed efficiently. Taking five minutes to contemplate the location of white wine bottles and the tastiness of fresh tomato is not asking much. Most Homestead cooks forego eating privileges in sacrifice of time constraints and the reigning supremacy of food cost. And most cooks would rather spend their time at the bar anyhow, masticating liquid nutrition rather than solid. Ebbi refuses to fall into this entrapment, taking full advantage of his access to food and the rights he has to relax after many hours of hard labor.

Just because Ebbi justifies his sandwich does not mean his co-workers will readily sympathize with him. Many look at Ebbi with grimacing faces of resentment. Sure, they would like to eat and relax as well, but they do not see that as an option. Ebbi's co-workers were already resentful when he grilled a piece of salmon before the shift began. Two food breaks in one night. Most cooks would never consider this an option. Line-cooks are afraid and intimidated to eat food from the kitchen they work for. Somehow, the ideology of political economics has convinced and intimidated cooks into fragmenting food from their own ingestion. Fragmenting them from the fruits of their own labor. Refusing food and drinking at the bar is preferred and safer for their identity. Management is very happy because they not only save food cost when cooks refuse to eat, but earn profit when the cooks pay for drinks at the bar.

Just as Ebbi took another bite of his finely constructed sandwich, Gregg returned to the kitchen with smoke trailing his feet. Noticing Ebbi's full mouth and leaned posture, he tried to ignore his impatience for laziness by mentioning something to Wendy as she passed by. A word about inventory, most likely a word making Wendy take note of it on her clipboard before strutting off to the cellar. The kitchen crew grew quiet as the chef entered, working harder and busier than when he was absent. Except for Ebbi. Ebbi was not much affected by Gregg's entrance, and did not change his behavior at all. Still leaning and eating his sandwich the same as he was, Ebbi remained comfortable and confident in his relaxed position.

Ebbi rightfully earned a few minutes at the end of shift to enjoy the fruits of labor he usually gives to customers. Customers who are anonymous and distant. A faceless public feeding off Ebbi's labor without reciprocating eye contact. However, even if Ebbi is justified, there are written rules and etiquette to follow, as well as implied rules and ideology to internalize without explicit direction. According to written law, all workers are suppose to have designated break times to relax and fill their bellies. Not during cleanup. According to implied law, workers are never to slouch no matter how justified they may be.

Ordinarily, the sight of Ebbi leaning on a counter top would not be cause for alarm. Ebbi has a habit of doing this while everyone else is still working. Usually Gregg does not come back into the kitchen after retiring to his office, and does not witness Ebbi in his leaning position. But this time he did. The other workers knew something was wrong, and tried to clue Ebbi of his monitored actions, using silent eye contact to conduct this delicate communication. It didn't work. Ebbi continued to lean and eat, chewing even slower and more deliberately than he had before.

Gregg's attitude turned to annoyance because all other workers were scampering about, cleaning while Ebbi remained eating. Little did Gregg know Ebbi had finished all his work faster than they, working more efficiently and thoroughly than it appeared. All Gregg saw was Ebbi slacking on the clock. Bureaucracy doesn't always care much for practical reality of things to be, but rather the image of things being. Workers ought to always be in motion.

"Ebbi, make sure the shrimp is covered, and the mushrooms are put away. I don't want to find them on the sauce shelf again like I did last week", Gregg confronted Ebbi's leaning with an order of oversight.

"Already done. And the mushrooms were left on the sauce shelf by someone other than me, because it happened on my day off. But I will make sure it never happens again, never threatens our system's efficiency", Ebbi said in defiance of unnecessary oversight, even though his tone remained soft and laconic.

"Just make sure it doesn't happen again. We can't function in a kitchen full of chaos. And don't forget about sloppiness, because sloppiness can reek havoc on cross contamination and unwelcomed critters", Gregg reiterated the politically correct words of a bureaucrat. He mostly intended the words to be the last on Ebbi's matter, to have the final say over one of his subordinate employees. Whether wrong or right, out of line or inside, chefs don't like to be told they're wrong and challenged by subordinate workers. And they especially don't like to be told the final word. Even if the subordinate worker is justified, chefs do not like to be shown heresy to their power of dominance, which is a dominant reason why bureaucracy so often follows erred paths.

"I found sliced fruit for the smoked salmon plate sitting next to raw chicken today. Our restaurant would have been shut down had the inspector decided to pay us a visit. Weren't you the one slicing fruit today, Gregg?" Ebbi took an offensive dig at his fearless chef.

Gregg tried to ignore the comment, but it was too late. He had already heard it and could not walk away without responding and still expect to keep his dignity. Gregg had only initiated the conversation with Ebbi as an indirect way of expressing displeasure with leaning and eating, and now it backfired into an exposure of ignorance. Gregg did not appreciate this exposure, and his anger at Ebbi grew. Indeed, it was a very hazardous comment to make. Gregg had only placed the fruit somewhat adjacent to the chicken because the cooling cheesecakes had taken up too much room for it to fit anywhere else. He forgot to move the fruit back into their correct position after the cheesecakes were finished cooling. He forgot, but Ebbi remembered.

"Ebbi, finish up your sandwich and get moving with cleanup. You're still on the clock, and you're stealing payroll money from this restaurant when you lean. If you've got work to do, do it. If not, punch out and get out. There's no leaning on the job at our Homestead, we're here to accomplish goals of efficiency. And the last time I checked, no instruction manual ever listed slacking as an admirable characteristic of a competitive kitchen", Gregg responded the only way he knew how. To attack him from a position of authority instead of reason.

"I'm almost done. I gave this restaurant 71/2 hours of hard labor this evening, and the least it can do is grant me five minutes to finish a sandwich. I didn't get a chance to take a break today, I was too busy and there wasn't enough time to do so. This is the only chance I got. My stomach is growling for the food it needs, and you ought to be happy, for these five minutes are a small price to pay for the labor I give this restaurant", Ebbi angered Gregg even more, as he enunciated the ignorance of not only the chef, but the restaurant as well.

"Just be happy it wasn't 81/2", came Gregg's reply. A meager response it was.

"This restaurant doesn't let me work 81/2 because they don't want to pay me overtime. I just do my job like I'm asked, without complaining. All I ask is five minutes at the end of a shift to enjoy a sandwich. Is that too much to ask, given the dedication I bring to the Homestead?" Ebbi was now walking on thin ice with the chef.

What started out as something simple has turned into a fiasco Gregg wants nothing to do with. If Ebbi had just closed his mouth, literally, and complied to chef's orders, none of this would have escalated into the situation it was swiftly becoming. Ebbi could have finished his sandwich and been well on his way out the door.

"Ebbi, stop talking and finish your work. Its been a long day, and I don't feel like arguing about stupid things. Just finish your sandwich and clock out. It's too late to be speaking of such insignificant matters", Gregg said as he stepped toward his office. He was trying to leave but could not manage the final word over Ebbi he insisted upon.

"Stupid things? You think my words are stupid? This is by far the most important conversation we have ever discussed here at the Homestead. You can't give a few inches of relaxation to one of your most dedicated employees to eat a sandwich? Do you know how ridiculous you sound? We give you 71/2 uninterrupted hours of labor, and five minutes is asking too much? I'm sorry if I'm ingesting your precious food cost, but deal with it. With all the money this restaurant profits off my labor, it can afford an avocado, a tomato and some bread. Don't make me into some kind of criminal for taking what I have rightfully earned, because punishment for this crime will be difficult to remedy. I only seek what I rightfully earn, and right now I have earned leaning rights over this counter top", Ebbi was now speaking with an inspired tongue as the avocado slid down his throat.

Gregg was not expecting such a reaction from his best sauté cook, expecting only reluctant compliance to his authority. But now the flames of conflict had been fanned, and they were about to expose many more conflicts in the Homestead kitchen.

Gregg now spoke directly to Ebbi, saying, "I have always held my tongue over your pestering of the wait staff. Ebbi, nobody cares where vegetables come from or how fish fins point upward for better direction control. They only care about taking food products to their customers in a timely fashion. The wait staff has complained about this harmless but annoying pestering, but I have always defended you. I have always defended your passionate love and respect of food. I find it charming, although impractical and extraneous. I don't want to see our efficiency slow down due to explanations of the political dangers of genetically enhanced foods, but I'm willing to tolerate it because it shows ebullience otherwise difficult to denude in most other people. Don't discredit my lenient tolerance for your passion. Consider this before acting on insubordination towards your chef." Gregg ripped into Ebbi with precise and well timed words, fierce enough to attack but delicate enough to maintain respect and dignity.

"Well, have you heard of soil branding and diminishing seeds? It's a very important issue, and one to affect our American lives for many years to come. How else am I to express my social consciousness and passion for food if I cannot use the appropriate words to satiate my expression? I would think it a crime to say nothing", Ebbi replied with ardent fervor in his voice.

"Nobody wants to be bothered with consciousness and passion when so many other distractions reign supreme. You have to let them serve food without worrying about the present turmoil in our food supply. We don't sell consciousness, Ebbi. We sell food products. People are eating, stomachs are full, money is exchanged, all are happy. Keep it that way. Nobody has time for political views or passionate food preparation. Just do what you are told, and try not to rock the boat", Gregg was now involved on a much deeper level. No longer merely trying to get the last word, Gregg now conjured his own passions.

"But knives are suppose to be kept sharp, avoiding injuries to the spirit of food. Dull knives without precise cuts can corrupt the spirit inherent to vegetables and fish. Don't laugh at me when I speak of such spirits. Spirits are alive, and we must take strides to assure their vivacity in support of future potential. Food is a metaphor for existence", Ebbi now felt a cause much deeper than defending his lean and eat.

Gregg responded as the entire kitchen listened in on the confrontation. "Sure it's important. But not to the immediate business of running a restaurant. We sell food here, not metaphoric philosophy. If you want to talk philosophy, go be a professor and philosophize all day long in doctoral theses. But while you're here, make the food and stop talking so much."

"Philosophy is life. It is the spirit of thinking. Confining it to words in a book is committing a crime against human nature. Philosophy is relevant, philosophy is dynamic. Don't trivialize my thoughts, for you will be injuring philosophy as well as yourself."

"Ebbi, stop talking and get back to work. That's my point. You're only procrastinating compliance to my orders. Nobody has time to philosophize with you during work hours, and the time clock can't afford any extraneous activity away from immediate business. The business of food products is more important than the spiritual essence of life. Stop leaning and eating, finish cleaning, punch out, and go home. Time is money, and right now you are wasting both."

"Time and money are parts of the efficient system, not the basis. With envisioned passion and inspired action, the Homestead could be made into a beacon of metaphor for all human spirits. It's our food, chef. We have the opportunity to showcase the metaphor of food. Life is food. Food is life. Don't let relevance fall into fragmented pieces of sterile bureaucracy. Act now while future potential still exists in the hearts and minds of our community and has not fallen by the wayside."

"Ebbi, maybe one day you will understand how the world works. Ideals are fun to talk and dream about, but they don't work in practical reality. Don't hold up the progress of bureaucracy with fantasy."

"I do speak of bureaucracy. Don't you see? Don't you see how spirits can be destroyed and left to rot when not taken care of, when not nourished with the philosophy of metaphor? Our collective lives hang in the balance of life and death, and you are willing to rot them for the value of money? The value of bureaucratic process! Don't you see the future potential we could pursue in this restaurant? Our bureaucracy has the potential of spiritual satiation if we just led our lives with more conscious relevance to common sense and practical reality. Don't you see American future potential to become more conscious versions of our own spirit?"

"No. Now finish your work and get going. I don't want to see you taking up any more time on the clock. Your sandwich is done, now start fulfilling those bureaucratic values you speak of and get out," came an impatient reply from the chef.

"If you can't see the passion of spirit I speak of, and the future potential enlaced in our community to satiate spirits, then let me be the leader to show the people metaphor. I do not profess ideals without relevant practical reality to accompany. Our definitions of practical reality exist on two different ends of the spectrum, and do not judge me according to yours. I am no pessimist, nor an optimist without a sense of reality. I can structure a menu based on a philosophy of food to change the ideology of the world and fill bellies with delicious and satiating consciousness," Ebbi replied with widening eyes.

"We can't run a restaurant without serving the people what they want. Nobody would come. You can't make a menu of foods you want people don't want because the public will not respond. People don't like having their independent choices taken away from them."

"Then you are saying people choose to suffer with their emaciating lives? If people ever had an independent power to choose as you have suggested, why don't they choose passion? If people could truly choose what they wanted, passion would be overflowing in the communities of our entire nation. People are not choosing what they truly want, because they don't actually have this choice. They follow the path bureaucracy has laid for them. I intend to give people a choice of consciousness, not merely indulge them in the choices that have lead them to spiritual emaciation. The choice of health and longevity. The choice of spiritual satiation. These are the real choices. Trust the future potential of humanity. I will show the people they have been inhaling tar fumes all these years, and provide a whiff of fresh air. I will not change them. I will merely inspire them to become more conscious versions of their own spirit."

"Look, stop with the talk and get back to work. I wanted you to stop leaning and eating so you could start working again, not to continue talking and avoiding work. Now let's go. I'm not kidding anymore," as Gregg became more impatient with Ebbi.

"I'm not avoiding work, I want to work. I do work. Very hard. Don't avoid inspiration. The potential flavors to come from this kitchen could be of divinity, for they would not be limited to the sweet, bitter, and salty of tongue. They would be flavors of spiritual expression, of ardent passion and the yearning for future potential to become reality where now it suffers under a veil of ignorance. The food would not merely warm the palate with wonder, but warm the spirit to radiate satiation across and within our humanity," as Ebbi's heart started racing.

"You're crazy. People would never sacrifice their comforts. Your restaurant of passion would never take off the ground, it would fail before the first customer walked out the door in disgust. It would stumble immediately. Money would be something your restaurant would not have. People wouldn't eat there. Prices would be too high to serve organic vegetables instead of pesticide riddled genetically enhanced produce, maple syrup instead of processed corn syrup, food products free of preservatives and product enhancing additives, and chickens raised without chemical hormones. It just isn't possible for a restaurant to run like your dreams have constructed. The bureaucracy of our nation is too powerful to operate without it. Someday you will wake up and accept reality for what it is, and realize the impossibility of changing the world. The public is too stubborn and comfortable in their ways, and decisions are led by wallets, not passion."

"Impossible? No, never. Passion is always possible. Passion will trump wallets once passion is made conscious and visible. I am going to grow vegetables in a garden, and replace processed food products of factorized food purveyors with dignified human labor. No more frozen processed garbage, our food will be hand spun and stamped with dignity," as Ebbi became even more inspired with passionate words.

"Well, you try and coordinate people to work like that. It's not as easy as it sounds. People enjoy comforts and preferences, and even if you think these comforts and preferences are unconscious and injurious, this is the way reality exists, because this is the way people want it to be. You can't change people, especially when it comes to their money, and more especially when it comes to their food," as

Gregg was now more involved in this conversation than he ever wanted to be.

"I don't want to change people. I want to inspire them. Inspire them to dig deeper into life and uncover the consciousness of their own existence. All the answers are here, people just need the tool to dig them out."

"Well, good luck. But until then, get back to work. The bureaucracy does not wait for people to finish eating before demanding its intentions. While you may inspire people through philosophy, I inspire bottom lines through monetary profit. My system works. I can't make any profit with you leaning on a counter top, so get back to work."

"All right. I'll get back to work. And someday, I will be able to cut through the bureaucracy limiting the emergence of satiated spirits. Someday, we'll be able to cut through the confusion repressing the sprout of future potential. Someday we will be able to cultivate the consciousness of practical reality, cutting through the bureaucracy of future potential to satiate our doorways of the cosmos to higher plateaus. Someday, the bureaucracy of future potential will become a beacon of passion."

www.ingramcontent.com/pod-product-compliance
Lightning Source LLC
Chambersburg PA
CBHW020610250626
47154CB00004B/1449